The Frannie Shoemaker Campground Mysteries
Bats and Bones
The Blue Coyote
Peete and Repeat
The Lady of the Lake
To Cache a Killer
A Campy Christmas
The Space Invader
We Are NOT Buying a Camper! (prequel)

The Time Travel Trailer Series
The Time Travel Trailer
Trailer on the Fly

the
TIME TRAVEL
Trailer

KAREN MUSSER NORTMAN

COVER DESIGN BY WICKED BOOK COVERS

*Dedicated to those who love vintage trailers,
especially the Midwest Glampers and
the Sisters on the Fly*

TABLE OF CONTENTS

Chapter One   1

Chapter Two   6

Chapter Three   12

Chapter Four   19

Chapter Five   25

Chapter Six   28

Chapter Seven   33

Chapter Eight   40

Chapter Nine   45

Chapter Ten   51

Chapter Eleven   56

Chapter Twelve   61

Chapter Thirteen   64

Chapter Fourteen   70

Chapter Fifteen   76

Chapter Sixteen   81

Chapter Seventeen   88

Chapter Eighteen   91

Chapter Nineteen   95

Chapter Twenty   99

Chapter Twenty-One   103

Chapter Twenty-Two   110

Chapter Twenty-Three   116

Chapter Twenty-Four   125

Chapter Twenty-Five   131

Chapter Twenty-Six   134

Chapter Twenty-Seven   139

Chapter Twenty-Eight   145

Chapter Twenty-Nine   151

Chapter Thirty   156

Chapter Thirty-One   161

Chapter Thirty-Two   166

Chapter Thirty-Three   171

Chapter Thirty-Four   180

Chapter Thirty-Five   187

Chapter Thirty-Six   194

Chapter Thirty-Seven   202

Chapter Thirty-Eight   211

Chapter Thirty-Nine   216

Chapter Forty   227

Chapter Forty-One   236

Chapter Forty-Two   242

Trailer on the Fly   246

Thank You   247

Acknowledgments   248

Other Books by the Author   249

About the Author   252

CHAPTER ONE

THE BATTLE BEGAN, as many do, with a skirmish. There was little indication at that point what direction the war would take.

"I don't want to go camping. I can stay with Dad."

"Dinah, it's just a suggestion. I thought it was something we could do together." I looked at my daughter's face, peering from behind a tangled curtain of blond hair and in a perpetual pout since she turned fourteen.

Dinah flung her hair back. I want to take a scissors to it when she does that. "If you want to do something together, why don't we go to the Mall of America? You're the hotshot travel agent. Aren't you supposed to please the customer?"

I sighed. I seemed to be doing that a lot lately. "Never mind. As I said, only a suggestion."

Dinah persisted. "What's wrong with the Mall of America?"

"Nothing's wrong with it but I wanted to do something where we could spend more time together—the two of us."

Now Dinah looked at me as if I had recently landed, and not from anywhere on this planet.

"Never mind. I know I don't want to tent camp and the trailers I looked at are pretty expensive, even used ones. Plus I'd have to buy a truck or something to pull it."

"You already looked for one? This isn't a discussion—you've already decided."

Now I was on the defensive as the volley heated up. "No, I haven't decided anything. Just wanted to see what kind of money was involved. Forget it."

For the first time that day, she did as I asked and returned to her phone, tuning me and my stupid ideas out as her thumbs flew across the keys. I was sure I wasn't getting good parenting reviews in that message.

To say that Dinah has not reacted well to my trial separation from Kurt would probably get me fined for understatement, if that is possible. To Kurt and me, the need to stand back and reassess our marriage was obvious. And it wasn't like Dinah was unaware of our growing rift. In the last year, Kurt had alternated between demanding and pleading, with increasing passion, for me to curtail or even end my career as the owner of a travel business, and with equal fervor I had resisted his demands. But we agreed that civility was an absolute must in dealing with Dinah and that we calmly tell her what was going to happen. That exemplary behavior was wasted on her.

We had taken her out to dinner at her favorite fast-food taco place and when we returned home, sat in the living room and explained that we are at odds on our life goals right now and that it would be best for all of us if we 'take a break' as they said on *Friends*.

As I said, the calm and logic was fruitless. It's not like she isn't well acquainted with similar situations through her friends. But she exploded. After sweeping the books off the coffee table, screaming at us both, and threatening to get 'Abandoned' tattooed on her right ankle, she stormed to her room.

Since then, it is anybody's guess what mood she may be in at any given time. Kurt reports that she doesn't spare him either. I find myself wondering what Rosemary's baby was like when he became a teenager. Don't get me wrong; I love Dinah and worry constantly about how to deal with her. My mother has always said that I cloak my worries in humor and sarcasm, and she's right.

Because I often think of Dinah as she was a few years ago. Fun and funny, eager to try new things, concerned about other people. She enjoyed spending time with both Kurt and me. No, really—no one is *that* good an actor. The teenage years roll around, those hormones kick in, and the Dogs of Hell are unleashed.

It's very difficult to talk to a teen these days. If no friends are around, there's always the phone, TV, iPods and video games for competition. So when a client came in for help with a family trip to Disney World, and ironically told me what wonderful times his family had had camping in the past, I started thinking that maybe I needed to get Dinah away from all of the distractions on a regular basis. But as I had told her, tents were out and the RV market, plus the required accoutrements, was too rich for my bank account. Somehow the Mall of America seemed like a stretch for fostering togetherness, however. I honestly felt that if I hit the right combination of approach and activity, I could bring our relationship back to where it had been a couple of years earlier. Yeah, right.

Dinah came back downstairs and dropped her duffle bag on the floor by the door. Headphones ringed her neck and her cellphone was, as always, attached to her hand. Kurt was coming by after work to pick her up for the weekend. I hoped she had calmed down a little or was even slightly remorseful. No such luck.

"You don't even *want* to get back together with Dad. It's over, isn't it?"

I was making myself a sandwich for supper and could have scraped the scorn off the floor with the knife.

I looked at her a minute, trying to decipher where she was coming from.

"Why would you say that? Neither of us knows what's going to happen."

"This camper business. Dad hates camping or doing outdoorsy things. If you were serious about working things out, you wouldn't be thinking about that!"

"Dinah, I told you that it was just a suggestion, which you rejected, so I've dropped it."

"But you would have done it if I agreed."

I threw up my hands, as Kurt honked in the driveway. "I promise you, if your dad and I can work things out, whether or not I buy a camper will not be a factor either way."

She rolled her eyes and slammed her way out of the door without even a good-bye. I looked at my sandwich and dumped it down the garbage disposal.

I spent the evening in front of the TV but even though a couple of my favorite shows were on, I couldn't tell you what they were about. I constantly replayed the earlier scenes with Dinah in my head and tried to come up with a way to make her see how unreasonable she was being. And how much better things could be if she only cooperated. The improbable plots on the TV shows were more likely.

It wasn't the first time I cried myself to sleep.

CHAPTER TWO

THINGS SEEMED BETTER in the morning, just as my grandmother always told me they would be. That was fitting, since both my mother and grandmother grew up in this house. It isn't large. Just a white frame house with living room, dining room, kitchen, and bath downstairs and two bedrooms under the eaves upstairs. It was a beautiful spring morning and the sun streamed in the east window. I had tossed and turned so long the night before that now I had overslept.

Saturdays at home are a luxury for me. Often I am gone guiding tours or in recent years at one of Dinah's soccer games. This spring, obviously in attempt to punish us, she announced that she was quitting soccer. But this morning, I needed to get a casserole out to Ben Walker, an older farmer in our church. Ben had been a friend for many years and I occasionally took him something for his supper. The casserole was done and in the fridge; it wouldn't take long to deliver, but I had told Ben I would have it there by 10:00 so that he wouldn't have to wait around if he had plans.

When I pulled into Ben's drive, he was sitting on the porch in an old swing, a mug of coffee in his hand. In a typical farmer wave, he raised one finger from the hand holding the mug and gave a barely perceptible nod. But, by the time I reached the front steps, he was at the top to greet me with a big smile.

"Hey, young lady! You're looking good this morning!"

I loved Ben. He always called me 'young lady.' I held up the casserole.

"Can I put this inside for you?"

"Follow me. Have you got time for a cup of coffee, Lynne?"

"Sure."

Soon we were back on the porch, seated side by side on the swing, mugs in hand.

"You have a beautiful view out here."

Ben nodded. "Minnie and I used to sit out here every morning. Even if it's raining — if the wind's not blowing — it's pleasant."

I had heard Ben talk of his wife Minnie but never knew her. He had told me once that she died shortly after a terrible car accident in the early 1960s. I looked over the rolling fields beyond the yard. Some were still covered with old cornstalk rubble, evidence of no-till practices, while others looked freshly plowed, the dirt as black as only the Midwest offers.

"Do you still farm any of your land?"

"No. I rent it out. The last few years these old bones won't do that kind of work any more."

He was so accepting of the trials in his life. I had never heard him complain.

"Have you ever thought about traveling?"

"Naw—too old for that too, I guess."

My eyes wandered to the old barn across the drive from the house. It was a beautiful building, weathered boards above a stone foundation. The entire farmstead was mowed and well trimmed, probably something Ben could still do. Or perhaps he had help. On the side of the barn away from the road, though, dead weeds as tall as a man surrounded some sort of structure.

I pointed. "What is that behind the barn?"

Ben laughed. "That's a real antique. It's a 1937 Covered Wagon. I should get rid of it."

I was confused. "A covered wagon? From the Thirties?"

"A camper trailer—Covered Wagon was the brand. They only made them in the Thirties and my dad bought it new."

"No kidding? A camper? Did you and Minnie ever use it?"

"We did after we were married in 1955, but after the accident Minnie was in a wheelchair and it got harder and harder to get her in and out. After she died, I didn't have much interest in it."

I shook my head. "She must have been quite a woman."

Ben rubbed his forehead and wiped an eye. "She was an amazing woman. She never let things get her down." He straightened up and the old Ben was back. "Anyway, we had some great times in it. Want to see it?"

"I'd love to."

"I'll get the keys. I keep it locked so kids don't think it's a good place to drink beer."

I followed Ben to the side of the barn and helped him pull some of the weeds away from the door. The trailer was a rectangular box, dark brown with a tan roof and several windows. The corners were rounded and the sides were smooth. He worked the key in the lock and finally got the door open.

Inside the walls and the ceiling were covered with wallpaper with green, orange, and yellow stylized flowers—very 60s looking. One end had a table with benches on either side. Kitchen cabinets and a wooden icebox took up the center and a couch extended across the front end. Avocado green carpet covered the floor.

"We put new cushions in it and then never used it again. There's even a bathroom," Ben said, opening a small door to reveal a tiny sink and chemical toilet. "No shower, though."

We went back outside. "This is amazing. What kind of truck does it take to pull it?" I felt pretty knowledgeable after my visits to two RV dealers.

"Truck? Nah. You can pull this with your car." He eyed my beloved old Jeep. I had a newer compact SUV but used the Jeep for all my trips around town.

"Really? How much do you want for it?"

He squinted at me. "Now *you're* kidding."

"No, seriously. I love it." And I told him about my plan to get Dinah off in the wilderness and back to her old self.

9

He looked skeptical. "I admire what you're trying to do, but don't count on too much, Lynne. Sometimes with teenagers, you just have to grin and bear it. But if you really want to try camping, you can have this."

"Oh, no, I couldn't take it. I'm sure it's worth a lot as a collector's item."

"I would rather someone was enjoying it than to have it sit in a museum. How about $200?"

We dickered and finally Ben agreed to take $500 for it. "Let's go in the barn. I'll find the hitch and you can have it installed on your car or your Jeep. It's a smaller sized ball than the ones they use now. Actually, I kept the camper in the barn until last summer and then had to make room for some other stuff. Way too much stuff." He grinned. "So the camper's been protected all these years and I just had to put new tires on it when I moved it outside."

He gave me the hitch and I put it in the back of the Jeep.

"Minnie always thought it would make a nice guest house — or an office."

My head snapped up. "What a great idea!" Rationalization was dawning. If Dinah refused to cave to the camping idea, what better office could you have for a travel agency than a travel trailer? If I could get the zoning changed, I could have my office right by my house. That would solve a lot of my parenting issues, too. So either way this would be a good buy.

Three days later, after I had the hitch installed on the Jeep, I closed up early and drove to Ben Walker's to pick up the trailer. I hadn't said anything to Dinah. She had been fairly upbeat when she returned from the weekend with her dad and I had no desire to throw cold water on that. Now that I had an alternate purpose for the trailer, I wasn't so worried about her reaction.

Other than a vague feeling of an extremely large dog following me home, towing the trailer the few miles from Ben's farm was uneventful. The fun began after I pulled in the alley behind my house. I had never backed a trailer of any kind. I didn't know at that time that you first need to turn the steering wheel in the opposite direction that you want the trailer to go.

CHAPTER THREE

THE CRUNCH WHEN the jackknifing trailer came in contact with the rear of the Jeep brought my heart to my throat and Jeanne Patterson, my neighbor across the alley, to her fence. At that moment, she looked like Wonder Woman to me. Jeanne hauls her horses around the countryside in a much longer trailer than I was pulling. If anyone could help me, she could.

"*What* have you got?" Her eyes were wide with admiration. I gave her a brief version of the events and then pointed out the dents I had just added to both vehicles. Fortunately, neither was very noticeable.

"Oh, bummer. Want me to give you a quick lesson?"

"Please."

With Jeanne's help, I got the trailer backed in behind my garage without further damage. Then I gave her the nickel tour.

"This is just amazing," she said. "I didn't know you were into camping."

"Well, that remains to be seen. I would like to be if I can get Dinah interested. Otherwise, I'm thinking of making it my office."

"That would be cool, too." Jeanne ran her hand over one of the wood cabinet doors. Each one was closed with an icebox style latch. "Are you going to restore it?"

"What? You don't like this vintage wallpaper?"

"Actually I do, but it's the wrong vintage for the trailer. There's probably wood underneath. Do a search for the model on the Internet, Lynne. You might be able to find pictures of what this originally looked like."

"Good idea."

"Mom!" Dinah's shrill voice came from outside.

"Oh, oh. This won't be pretty."

Jeanne raised her eyebrows. "I take it Dinah's not excited about this."

"She informed me that she could stay with her dad if I wanted to take up camping. I haven't even told her that I bought this."

Well." Jeanne dusted off her hands. "I'll leave you to it."

I followed her out the door and thanked her again for her help. As she walked away, I turned to Dinah, who stood, hands on hips.

"I thought you were giving up on this stupid idea if I didn't want to do it."

"What do you really think about it?" I thought that was a pretty good effort at keeping things light. She didn't, and just scowled, waiting for me to explain my naughty behavior.

I told her about finding the trailer behind Ben Walker's barn and what a great deal he gave me on it.

"I'm thinking I can make it my office. Travel trailer — travel agency — get it?"

She rolled her eyes, which is by far her most common reaction to anything I have the nerve to say or do.

"I thought you wanted to go camping." In case I didn't remember what I was doing.

"I would love to but not by myself. Ben said his wife always thought it would make a great guesthouse or office. It certainly would be a lot more convenient for me to work out here than downtown. Want to see it?"

She shrugged her shoulders, but I could tell she was curious so I just returned to the door and she followed.

Once inside she eyed the wallpaper with disgust.

"Boy, is that ugly."

"I agree. I'll probably take that off."

She looked around. "You couldn't camp in this anyway. There's no where to sleep."

Hmmm. Maybe this was progress. I thought she'd pick up first on the lack of a TV.

"Actually the couch makes into a bed and the table folds down to make another one."

"Huh. Seems to me that if you make it your office it will just be easier for you to spend even more time at work."

I decided to be agreeable. "You could be right but I plan to see that doesn't happen."

"Good luck," she said and headed for the house. I wasn't sure if she meant on the remodel or controlling my work hours.

I DECIDED TO replace the cushions on the couch and dining benches first—a little OCD influence, I guess. In case I ever *did* camp in this trailer, I didn't relish sleeping on 50-year-old mattresses, even if they had never been used. I took the measurements down to our local upholsterer and brought home fabric samples. My online research revealed that upholstery in the Thirties tended to be solid colors or small prints, with bigger patterns usually reserved for curtains.

I had managed to peel up a corner of the wallpaper and found mint green paint underneath. But it did look like that paint was on wood. So in the hopes that it could eventually be returned to its natural state, I chose a small geometric pattern in red and brown for the cushions. Other than that, in the next couple of weeks, I didn't have time to do much work on my new find.

Meanwhile, the daffodils bloomed and faded while Dinah played trapeze artist on her mood swings, causing my heart to alternately swell with joy or plunge to the depths of despair. In her loquacious moments, she regaled me with the idiocies of her teachers and the awesome accomplishments of her classmates. (Her best friend, Tish, was getting a new iPhone!) More often, she disappeared into her room or camped in front of the TV, thumbs flying over her phone, and pretended to be an orphan being magnanimously supported by an anonymous and distant benefactor to whom she owed nothing. In these moods, her only communication with me was to ascertain the time and nature of meals or to challenge my progress on the folly in the back yard.

The day I picked up the new cushions after work and brought them home, she trailed me out to see how they were going to look. I stood them on end against the walls.

"Not too great with that wallpaper," she said.

"The wallpaper isn't staying."

"What about electricity and stuff?"

"I need to have an outdoor outlet installed out here."

She opened one of the overhead cabinets and peered in. She wrinkled her nose.

"Yeah," I said. "It's a little musty. I need to wipe them out."

"I could do that."

I managed to shut my gaping mouth before she turned around. "That'd be great."

"So are you going to take it camping at least once before you make it into an office?"

I shrugged. "Do you think I should?"

Her turn to shrug. "I dunno. Seems like you oughta. Cheyenne Fulton's family camps a lot at Parsons' Grove, I guess."

I wasn't sure if Cheyenne was a boy or girl. "That's not far. It would be pretty easy. Should we?" Making it clear that this would not be a solo venture on my part.

"When? Like this weekend?" She almost sounded eager. Maybe Cheyenne was a boy, or if not, had a cute cousin.

I tried to play it cool. "Well, I'd have to juggle a couple of things. I haven't really cleaned it and we have to stock it with a few things at least, even just for a weekend."

"There's some old sheets in my closet from my bunk beads."

"The Toy Story ones?"

"What difference does it make? It's just for a weekend." The attitude was returning.

Don't press your luck, Lynne, I told myself.

"You're right. They'd be fine. Well, if you'll wipe out the cabinets, I'll clean up the bathroom and the counters. First help me carry these old cushions out of here so we can put the new ones in place."

I took the back cushion off the couch and Dinah grabbed the seat cushion. I was almost out the door when I heard her say, "Wow."

I stopped and looked back. "What?"

"There's a secret compartment under here," she said, pointing to a cloth strap attached to the wooden platform.

I laughed. "Hardly secret. All of the benches have storage under them. These things are pretty well planned."

"What's in them?"

"I don't think anything. I haven't looked in that one but there's nothing under the dinette benches."

She put the cushion down and lifted the seat.

"A treasure chest," she said.

"What?" I set my cushion down.

"Well, a shoebox." She grinned. "It *could* be a treasure." She leaned over and pulled a tattered, faded shoebox out of the compartment.

"Open it! Maybe we can sell the trailer and go to Hawaii."

Dinah removed the lid. "Jewelry. It doesn't look valuable to me but it's cool." She pulled out a daisy pin with enamel leaves and held it up.

"I remember Grandma Linda wearing one of those," I said, referring to my mother. "I think there's a picture of her holding me as a baby and she has that on. That's definitely late '60s."

"I like this." Dinah pulled a bracelet of pink and green glass beads over her slim wrist.

"I should probably check with Ben and see if any of it has special meaning for him. If not, you can have it."

Dinah put the bracelet back in the box and linked her arm in mine as we returned to the house. My own little Jekyll/Hyde said, "This might be fun, Mom."

CHAPTER FOUR

THE NEXT DAY after school, we showed Ben Walker the box of jewelry and he said he didn't want it. He seemed pleased that Dinah was so taken with it. We shopped for groceries for the weekend and stocked the cabinets after Dinah cheerfully gave them a thorough cleaning. Dinah asked if she could take a friend along for the weekend, which I declined since I honestly didn't know what I was doing. She felt that was very poor reasoning and didn't speak to me for the next four hours.

She begged to have Kurt for supper on Thursday night so we could show him "our" new find. After I got off work, we made sure we stocked pillows, blankets, and the Toy Story sheets, a couple of changes of clothes, and basic toilet articles. We figured if worse came to worse, we could find a store or come back home.

We ended our roller coaster week by working together on a pot of spaghetti. Dinah practically bounced off the walls.

Kurt's voice came from the front door. "Hey, girls! Anyone home?"

"Daddy!" Dinah answered, and raced to the door. She was seven again. She pulled him through the house by the hand to the back door. "I'm going to show him my camper, okay, Mom?"

I nodded, and as I stirred the sauce, reflected that the camper had gone from *mine*, to *ours*, to *hers* in a very short time. Kurt raised his eyebrows at me as Dinah steamrolled him through the kitchen. The one thing we could always agree on was that Dinah had us both buffaloed.

OVER OUR PASTA and French bread, Kurt quizzed me about the trailer.

Then he said, "I'm no expert but I've never seen anything like that before. I bet you could get a pretty price for it."

"I don't plan to sell it. Ben only gave me the deal that he did because he thought we were going to use and enjoy it."

"But if it doesn't work out...if you and Dinah decide camping isn't for you..."

"Then I will use it for my office."

"I don't think we're—I mean, you're—zoned for commercial here."

"I can request a variance or find some place that is."

"But if you move it someplace else, that defeats the purpose of getting your work closer to home."

I laid my fork on my plate, a little harder than necessary. "I don't know, Kurt. If I have to get rid of it eventually, I will, but for now I think it has a lot of potential."

He held his hands up. Steam was starting to come out of Dinah's ears, and Kurt knows when to stop. "Sorry. I was just trying to say that I think it's really worth something."

With the situation defused, Dinah told him about the jewelry find. She displayed the pink-and-green bracelet on her wrist. Kurt made suitable admiring noises and declined dessert, stating that he had work to do that night. Dinah protested but was quickly distracted by a call from one of her friends.

I felt the stress level drop after Kurt left. There was still a niggling feeling that things could blow up with Dinah at any time before we got our camping trip under way, but that was par for the course.

I had found a source for block ice to keep our 1937 icebox operating but I would wait and put that in and stock the icebox shortly before we left. Our clothes were already loaded. This early in the spring we needed both sweatshirts and tees.

Adding to my concern about forgetting something— really, topping that concern—was the knowledge of my inexperience in towing anything anywhere. Parson's Grove is only about ten miles from home on a two-lane highway but once there, I would have to back the trailer in. We had checked out the campground earlier in the week. All of the sites were empty since it was so early in the season and most spots looked pretty doable, even for a novice, but still…

We planned to load the icebox right after school and work and take off. Dinah was already home, her backpack by the door, when I arrived.

"I'll just change clothes and we'll load the icebox," I said.

"I can start," Dinah offered.

"Great." I showed her where I had collected items on one shelf of the refrigerator. She got a box to haul them to the camper while I went upstairs to change. I was just coming back down the stairs when I heard the familiar "Mom!"

Now what? It didn't sound good, but with Dinah it might mean she had a paper cut or the camper had tipped over.

"What's the matter?" Obviously from her tone, something was.

"What about water? I turned on the faucet but there isn't any water!"

Relief washed over me. "We'll fill the tank when we get there. There's a hydrant right at the entrance to the campground." Funny how being able to solve a problem quickly makes you feel in command. For a moment anyway.

"What do you fill it with?"

"A hose. We just hook a hose to the hydrant."

"We threw our hose out a few weeks ago, remember? It had a big crack in it."

I slapped myself in the forehead. "And I was going to pick up a new one and never did. Crap. Okay, you make sure you have everything you want and I'll run down to the hardware store."

By the time I got back and stowed the new hose, Dinah had increased her stash in the camper to include enough makeup for a movie set, more video games, a stuffed penguin, and a box of candy bars. In the hopes of more bonding, I added a deck of cards.

I began the tedious process of backing the car up to the camper. Dinah willingly gave directions but her hand signals were as difficult to interpret as her moods. It took nearly an hour to get it lined up and hitched to my satisfaction. For experienced people it's probably five minutes.

Dusk was approaching as we pulled out of town. Dinah buried herself in her phone; the novelty and excitement had obviously worn off.

WE PULLED INTO the campground and I managed to locate the water hydrant in the twilight. While the tank was filling, we surveyed what we could see of the campground. Two campfires at the other end marked campsites in use, and near the entrance to the left we could easily see a large motorhome because white rope lights were laid on the ground around the RV and blue lights outlined the awning. Other than that, the place looked empty and since all of the sites were first come-first serve, we had our pick. Dinah walked down the road and returned to report that the third site on the right looked good to her and easy to back into. Plus, the small shower house was just a few sites beyond, shrouded by trees and shrubs.

I pulled past the site Dinah had picked and remembered to crank my wheels in the opposite direction. Jeanne would be proud.

It wasn't pretty but since the site was large and the camper small, I got it parked. I had made a checklist for our set up so I didn't forget something really obvious.

"Can we have a campfire tonight? What's for supper?"

I smiled. "You start the fire. There's firewood in the back of the car. I picked up fried chicken and sides so we could eat as soon as we got here. I'll warm it up."

"Awesome!"

Take-out was a rare treat at our house and fried chicken was her favorite. I set the little table with a couple of cafeteria trays I'd found in the back of a cupboard at home. If you're going to splurge on take-out, you might as well have plenty of room for it, right?

It was a perfect evening. After supper, we washed up the dishes and made up our beds. Then we sat out by the fire. Dinah talked about her career goal—to be either a vet or a fashion designer. We roasted a couple of marshmallows and both ended up with marshmallow spread across our faces. It really felt like I had my daughter back.

CHAPTER FIVE

WHEN I WOKE in the morning, daylight was just visible where the curtains didn't quite meet. I had slept well on the couch bed; the new cushions were an excellent investment. I savored the moment. As I said, I didn't have that many unscheduled Saturdays at home, and even when I did, there were plenty of chores waiting to be done. Here all I needed to do was a couple of simple meals. Thoughts of the camaraderie the night before with Dinah comforted me as well. Finally a craving for a good cup of coffee got me out of my cocoon.

I'd found an old percolator at a second hand shop. It only made about four cups, which was perfect. I felt like a kid in a playhouse as I made coffee in it and lit the burner on the small stove. Dinah sprawled on the dinette bed, still sound asleep.

I read a novel while the coffee gurgled and when it finished, filled a ceramic mug and took it and my book outside.

It was a beautiful early spring morning. I looked out to the woods behind the campground and then around the campsite. The trees were bigger than I had realized last night in the dark. As I surveyed the area near the entrance, I was surprised to see that the big motorhome was already gone. Perhaps someone was traveling the nearby interstate and just stopped for the night.

However, a small vintage trailer had pulled into another site near where the motorhome had been. Obviously I had slept very well because I hadn't heard a thing. I set my mug on the picnic table and decided to visit the shower house.

But as I approached the building, I stopped with a jolt. The building that Dinah and I had used the night before had been cement block and appeared fairly new. The women's side held two sinks, three toilet stalls, and two shower stalls.

Now, in the same spot, stood two wooden outhouses, one marked 'Men's' and one marked 'Women's.' I stood frozen. Slowly I scanned the entire campground again. The large trees that shaded all of the sites were old elms —I hadn't ever seen that many in one place in my lifetime.

I reluctantly used the outhouse and when I came out, my head was spinning—whether from the fragrance of the building or the total disorientation I was feeling, I wasn't sure. There had been campfires in two campsites at the far end of the campground the night before but only one was occupied now with a canvas tent. I walked slowly around the single road that looped the campground, trying to get my head around this.

I may have been mistaken about the trees in the dark and I suppose people do move in and out of these places in the night according to their circumstances. But nothing explained the outhouses.

As I neared the vintage trailer, a woman came out and nodded. She was dressed in crisp, tapered khakis and a plaid shirt with a brown cardigan arranged on her shoulders. On her feet, bright white sneakers defied the dirt around them. Her hair was neatly arranged in a French twist and she could have been the mother in a Sixties sit-com.

In my research online, I had read that many people took their vintage trailer restoration to the extent of wearing period clothing as well. This gal was serious.

"Good morning!" I said. "What a great camper. It's in wonderful shape."

She looked a little confused. "It's new."

I took that to mean that it was 'new' to her. "Well, it looks very nice."

I completed the loop and returned to my own trailer. I realized I had forgotten to register and pay for my site the night before. The campground was so small that there wasn't a full-time attendant and they relied on the honor system most of the time. At a kiosk near the entrance, a rack held registration forms and a locked box with a slit in the top was provided to deposit the forms and payment.

I took the form back to my picnic table and filled it out. The bottom part was to be torn off and slipped into a holder on a post by my site. I wrote in my name and the site number. Blanks were provided to fill in the dates of my stay. The year was already filled in. It said '1962.'

CHAPTER SIX

 I SAT STUNNED, staring at that date. What was going on? This was awfully elaborate for a practical joke. More than that—it was impossible. No one replaces cement block shower houses overnight. Surely the county hadn't printed enough forms for fifty plus years. The door to the camper opened and Dinah came out in pajamas, a hoodie, and a scary nest of hair.

"Mornin'." She grumped and plopped in the other lawn chair.

Still in shock, I tried to bring myself back to the present—whenever that was.

"Sleep all right?"

"Um, yeah, good. Can't get any phone reception here. What's with that?" She looked at me. "Are you okay?"

"I don't know." There was no sense trying to avoid this. "Look around. Do you notice anything?"

She frowned at me, trying to determine if I'd finally gone over the edge, and looked around the campsite. "Nooo, what am I supposed to notice? Wait. Where did that tree come from?" She pointed to a large elm about ten feet from our fire ring. Except that the ring was gone and only a pile of ashes and scraps of wood lay in the middle of a large bare spot.

"What do you mean?"

"There weren't any trees on that side of the fire last night. We watched the moon come up, remember? And none of the trees were that big." She rubbed her eyes. "What is going on, Mom?" She looked frightened.

I leaned over and took both of her hands in mine. "Honey, something very odd is happening. I don't know what either. But remember when we walked to the shower house last night? Describe it to me."

"Describe it? It's just a shower house."

"What is it made of?"

"Cement, I suppose. What are you getting at?"

"Bear with me a minute. Running water?"

She scoffed. "Of course."

"Flush toilets?

"Mom, yes! What are you getting at?" she said again.

"Walk with me." I took her hand and she reluctantly came out of her chair. We went down the road far enough to see the shower house. But the two outhouses still stood in that spot.

Dinah gaped and clung to my hand. She looked at me but no words came and we returned to our campsite.

I continued to hold her hands while I told her what I had discovered. "Most of these trees are elms. Elms were pretty much wiped out in the Sixties by the Dutch elm disease. Remember the big motorhome that was over there last night?" I pointed to the other side of the entrance. "It's gone. It could have taken off in the night. But look at that trailer. It wasn't there last night. The lady told me it was 'new.' "

I pulled over the registration forms. "Look at this." I pointed to the year. "Honey, everything in this campground today points to it being the early Sixties."

She had started to cry and rubbed her eyes with her fists. "It's a nightmare, Mom. We're having a nightmare. Or one of us is."

"I hope so. But it doesn't feel like it."

"It feels like it to me."

I rubbed my forehead. "Let's go get dressed. And have breakfast. I've never eaten a meal in a nightmare."

She seemed in a trance and I couldn't blame her. We went inside and dressed in jeans and sweatshirts.

"I'm not very hungry," Dinah said.

"Me either, but we need to eat something. We have some little boxes of cereal."

I got out the pack of individual boxes that Dinah had thought were so cool when she was little. They weren't doing much for her now.

She had removed her sheets, folded them, and put the dinette back to its eating configuration. My daughter, who thinks that the proper disposal of a wet towel is on her bedroom carpet, was turning into Miss Tidy-house. I felt the same. We were both grasping at routine to restore our sanity.

We sat at the table facing each other.

"I wanna go home, Mom."

"Me too, in every sense of the word. But I think we should scout things out first."

Her eyes widened. "What do you mean?"

"After we eat, let's just take a ride. We'll drive back into town and see what we can see."

It dawned on her what I was saying. If things weren't the same here, maybe they weren't the same at home either. Maybe the world we knew was gone. If possible, the fear in her face increased and she reached across the table to clasp my hand again.

We rinsed out our dishes in silence and stacked them in the sink. Dinah picked up her cell phone while I grabbed the car keys. She punched a few buttons and looked at me dismally. "Still no signal."

"I'm not surprised."

Once we were in the Jeep and headed back to town, she seemed to relax a little. But she said, "Do you know what's going on and you just don't want to tell me?"

I shook my head. "It seems like some kind of a time warp but I don't believe such a thing exists."

She rode the rest of the way into town without speaking and gazed out the window with such longing that it made my heart break.

I wasn't hopeful. While the farms along the road didn't look all that different, all of the cars we met were 1960s or earlier. I was thankful that Jeeps had kept the same style for so long that our car didn't attract an undue amount of attention.

31

The city limits were closer in. The housing developments that had sprung up on the outskirts of town in the last forty years were still fields waiting to be plowed. As I drove slowly down the highway through town, I searched for anyone or anything that would indicate we were in the 21st century. Nothing.

I turned down our street. I knew we were in trouble when a man I had never seen before, wearing coveralls and carrying a lunch pail, came out of our front door. He headed for the light blue 1959 Chevy parked at the curb.

CHAPTER SEVEN

 I DROVE AWAY in shock.

"I'm scared," Dinah said, still watching the impostor who had taken over our house.

"Me too, a little." Perhaps a bit of an understatement.

"How do we get back?" She looked at me. Mom has all the answers, right?

"First we have to figure out how we got here."

"It must be the camper," Dinah said. "But we've been in it a lot for the last month and this never happened."

"The only thing we never did before is sleep in it," I said.

She nodded. "What do you think will happen if we sleep in it again? Will we go back home or to a different time?"

"Good question. You know, honey, I can't see that we are in any danger. So we need to stay calm and think about this logically."

"'Keep Calm and Carry On'?' she said with the first smile I had seen that day.

"Exactly. I can't help but feel there's a reasonable explanation."

"Really?" She must be feeling better; her sarcasm was back.

I shrugged. "Well...reasonable by somebody's standards."

We were headed back out of town to the campground, mostly because I didn't know what else to do. And because that's where the problem had started.

As we pulled back in, I could see a few people around the tent at the far end but no other activity. I was thankful it was so early in the season. It might save us from being asked a lot of questions that we couldn't answer.

"Let's go inside," I said. It was obvious to me that Dinah had no intention of staying outside by herself.

I turned on the burner to heat up my coffee and Dinah got a bottle of water out of the icebox.

"Best put that in a glass if you take that outside. I don't think bottled water was around in the Sixties."

"I know."

We sat at the table. How many times in her life we had sat at the kitchen table at home to discuss her behavior or Kurt's and my expectations. But nothing to compare with this.

"I don't know how we can make a plan. We don't know anything for sure."

I shook my head. "I don't think we can deny we are in a different time. 1962. It appears to be the same time of year—just a different year. Some things could be explained away: the change in campers overnight, the cars on the highway could be going to one of those classic

34

car rallies; maybe we don't remember exactly what the trees looked like in the dark. But the shower house and the guy coming out of our house—there's no other explanation."

"Why 1962?" Dinah said. "This camper is older than that. 1937, you said."

"I don't know. Maybe 1962 was the last year it was used? Ben did say that he and Minnie used it in the Fifties and Sixties." I noticed the pink and green bracelet on her wrist. "Did you have that on last night?"

She stared at it. "You think…?"

"Maybe. It's from the Sixties, I'm pretty sure."

She pulled it off and laid it on the table between us. We watched it almost as if it was a spider ready to spring. A knock at the door caused us both to jump.

I got up and went to open it a crack, trying to think of anything we had out that would cause question. The Toy Story sheets maybe; certainly Dinah's video game and my cell phone lying on the counter.

The woman from the small trailer stood on the steps.

"Hi! I hate to do this but was wondering if you possibly had some oleo I could borrow? I'm fixing lunch and my husband will be back soon and I forgot to bring any."

I heard a scramble behind me as Dinah grabbed the electronics. Good girl. I couldn't ask her to get the oleo— she probably wouldn't know what that was.

"Sure," I said and opened the door wider. "Step in."

She did and looked around, while I got a stick of margarine out of the icebox.

"Wow!" she said, looking around. "This is pretty old, isn't it?"

You don't know the half of it, I thought, but said, "It is. 1937. It was—um—my grandfather's."

"You've fixed it up nice though—great wallpaper."

I hoped she didn't notice Dinah's snort as I closed the icebox door with a thunk and handed her the margarine.

"Is that an old ice chest?"

"Yeah, it's original. It works pretty well actually. I'm Lynne, by the way, and this is my daughter, Dinah."

She held out her hand. "Nice to meet you. My name is Vicki Atherton. Are you from around here?"

Dinah started to speak and I cut her off. "No, actually, we're just passing through. We're from Ohio."

She raised her eyebrows. "Oh? I'm surprised. I thought I noticed a local license plate."

Damn. There's a year on the plate, too—I hoped she hadn't noticed that. I laughed, probably not convincingly. "Oh, we had big car trouble not far from here. I actually had to buy that Jeep on the spot. The—um—engine blew up in ours."

"That's terrible." She turned to go. "Well, thank you very much. This is a lifesaver. Jim has to have his oleo on his sandwich. See you later." And she was out the door.

Dinah barely contained her laughter. "Mother, you are *such* a good liar!"

I smirked at her. "I learned from you. You're a little truth-challenged yourself at times."

"Why didn't you want her to know we were from here?"

"I was afraid she would ask if we knew so-and-so or shopped at a certain store or something."

"Ohhh. Good point. Mom, I just thought of something else a minute ago. I thought your family owned our house for a long time. Who was that guy coming out of there?"

"You're right. Grandma Linda would have been…" I did some quick, probably inaccurate, mental math…"nine or ten in 1962."

"So was that guy your grandpa?"

"I don't think so. He didn't look anything like I remember. Besides, he appeared to have a blue-collar job and Grandpa was in sales."

"So…?"

"I don't know. We'll have to ask Grandma Linda when we get back."

"If we get back."

"Don't say that. But something I thought of when she mentioned the license plate—we need to smudge up the year somehow. The style has changed too, but there's nothing we can do about that."

Dinah's eyes grew wide. "Wow. There's so many things to think about. I'll do that." She grabbed some eye shadow out of her makeup kit. I knew that would come in handy.

"Don't let anyone see you."

"I'll be like the wind."

Where did she get that? She was back a few minutes later.

"I was very sneaky. I pretended I had to tie my shoe and while I was bent over, just reached over and—SWIPE! And speaking of shoes, did you see that lady's? *White*—I mean, whiter than white. Who would wear those?"

"Probably lots of people in 1962. Styles change, you know. Want a sandwich?"

"Yeah. I'll get the stuff out." She opened the icebox and rummaged around. "And she liked the wallpaper, too!"

"Well, somebody put it up to begin with. They must have liked it."

As I layered lunch meat, lettuce and cheese on whole wheat bread, I remembered my mother admonishing me: "Be careful what you wish for." I had wished for time alone with my daughter to rebuild our fragile relationship. I think I secretly wanted her to be more dependent on me again. Well, guess what! In a lot of ways, we were alone in the world. She was almost clinging to me. And was I sure I could allay her fears? No way, baby.

The buoyancy that had inflated her mood from Vicki's visit to the license plate fix fizzled out—I could see it in her face.

"What are we going to do, Mom?"

"We are going to get through the day with as little social interaction as possible, go to bed with no 1960s jewelry on, and see where we wake up tomorrow. Then we will panic." I smiled at her and handed her a sandwich.

"It's not funny."

"I'm well aware it's not funny but since there's nothing else I can do at this point, what does it hurt?"

"You need to take this seriously." She actually stamped her foot. Are we reversing roles here?

I put my arm around her. "I know." She broke down in sobs. "Let's eat our lunch and then play some cards. It'll help pass the time."

"I don't know how."

"Time to learn."

While we chewed our sandwiches, not tasting much, we stared out the windows. It was going to be a long afternoon.

CHAPTER EIGHT

I TAUGHT DINAH a couple of simple card games and then she said she thought she would take a nap.

"Okay, but I'm not going to let you sleep too long because we need to sleep tonight. Take the couch." I got my book and sat at the dinette to read. It was very difficult to concentrate and I finally gave it up.

I have never been an aficionado of fantasy or time travel literature. I remember seeing a couple of science fiction movies as a kid that involved traveling through time in elaborate, whimsical machines. Not much help here. No dials to set that I could see. I decided to look under the dinette benches, but found nothing. Did Ben Walker know about this? I couldn't imagine that he would have not told me. Of course I wouldn't have believed him. But if he had known, why let me buy it? I convinced myself that he didn't know anything about it.

I opened a couple of empty cabinets and peered inside. Nothing there either.

Dinah stirred and opened one eye. "What are you doing?"

"Just looking to see if there's something about this trailer that we missed. You didn't sleep long."

"I can't. Too scared."

"I know. But we'll be okay. I'm sure of it."

"How?" She sat up. "What if we never see Daddy or Grandma Linda again? Or my friends?" She was close to tears again. I didn't want to point out that maybe she could get to know her grandmother as an annoying ten-year-old.

I sat down beside her and pulled her close. "I know I said we should avoid everyone else if we can but I think we need to get some fresh air. Let's go out and take a walk. There's some nice hiking paths in this park. Remember when we had the church picnic here a few years ago?"

She smiled a little now at catching me in a slip-up. "That wasn't a few years ago. That was about fifty years from now."

"You're right. But we'll get away from the campground and see what we can find." I pulled her up. "Get your shoes on."

Once we were ready, I opened the door a little to make sure no one was in the immediate vicinity. Outside, we walked away from the campground and toward the woods. As we skirted the woods, we looked for signs denoting hiking trails but apparently the county wouldn't be posting those for a few years yet. However, we soon came to the entrance of a well-worn path that led downhill through the trees.

Dinah led, and to my surprise, I found that my proposed remedy was spot on. The crisp spring air was clearing my head and lifting my spirits. Maybe this *was* just a nightmare. The problem was that I didn't remember ever thinking a dream was just that while it was going on. But then I didn't always remember all of my dreams. Going in circles.

The trail led down to a stream moving swiftly with spring runoff. Dinah found a couple of stones to pitch into the current. I sat on a fallen log and watched. Some crashing through the brush downstream startled us and heralded the arrival of a young boy, probably nine or ten.

"Hi!" he said, spotting us.

"Hi yourself," Dinah said. I breathed a sigh of relief — we probably wouldn't have to explain ourselves or watch what we said so closely as we would around an adult.

"Whatcha doin'?" he said, and at the same time, searched for a rock he could throw.

"Nothing," Dinah said. "What're you doing?" She threw a rock at a small log floating down the stream.

"Hunting Russians."

Dinah stopped and looked at him. "Did some escape?"

He shrugged. "Can't be too careful. My dad says President Kennedy is too weak and won't stand up to 'em. He says they'll take over the country. I figure this would be a good place for 'em to hide." He looked very serious.

Dinah kept a straight face. "Well, good luck."

"Is that your mom?" He pointed at me.

"Yeah."

"Can't you come out by yourself?"

"I can if I want. But I'm afraid of the Russians." She looked back at me and rolled her eyes.

"Ohhh," he said and nodded. "I better keep hunting."

"Be careful," Dinah called after him.

"I will."

"Ready to go back?" she said to me.

I smiled. "I think so. Nice to have a little entertainment."

We headed back up the trail. "Were people that afraid?" Dinah asked.

"I guess some were. Too bad we can't tell him that in six months Kennedy will make the Russians back down."

"Really?"

"The Cuban Missile Crisis was in October of 1962."

"Oh, yeah, we studied that in history."

WE PLAYED A couple more games of cards when we got back and then started a small fire to cook some hamburgers for supper. It was a pleasant evening, too early for bugs. A fiery red sunset bathed the campground in a pink glow while we cooked. We spoke very little.

I got out a bag of chips, and we laid out our simple supper on the dinette inside, again to avoid conversation or questions, even though the campground was still mostly empty. It was hard to fight the impending feeling of doom.

"We need a TV," Dinah said as she settled on the couch after we did up the dishes and stowed them back in the cupboards.

"No antenna," I said. "I doubt if we'd get any reception."

"We could put cable in."

"No cable in 1962."

"Oh."

We both got out our books and read in fits and starts, interspersed with fidgeting and looking out the windows. Finally, I said, "Think you can go to sleep?"

She shrugged, but got up and started making the dinette into her bed. I did the same and soon I gave her a long hug and we crawled into our Toy Story sheets, desperately hoping for a return to normal—our normal.

CHAPTER NINE

SLEEP WAS A long time coming, and then I woke up a couple of times. I was afraid to get up and look out. In the middle of the night, Dinah came and crawled in with me. We clung together, both for comfort and of necessity—even opened up, the couch was barely wider than a twin bed.

I had dozed off again when a change in the darkness awoke me. A bright spot of light came through the gap in the curtains and at first I thought it must be morning. Then I remembered that the first night, a security light at the entrance coming through the curtains had annoyed me as I tried to go to sleep.

Nervous and excited, I climbed over Dinah and looked out the window. Sure enough, the security light that had not been there in 1962 illuminated the entrance and the large motorhome across the way.

None of the phrases used to describe relief—a great weight lifting, a load off my mind, a silver lining—covered what I was feeling. I looked at my watch—it was only 4:30 but I was sure I wouldn't get back to sleep. I turned on the little light over the dinette bed and as quietly as possible, put a pot of coffee on.

With a restoring mug of coffee, I sat on the dinette bed and peeked out of the window. Even in the dark, I could tell that the huge elms were gone, replaced by ash and maples of more moderate size. I was confident that if I wandered down the road, I would find the cement block shower house with lovely flush toilets.

As my emotions settled, I began to wonder about other ramifications. Had the camper and truck remained in the present as well as being in the 1962 campground? Or had it disappeared with us? If so, what questions would that raise with other campers?

I set the empty mug on the counter and lay down. I didn't think I could go back to sleep but I was wrong. I awoke again to Dinah shaking me.

"Mom! Mom! We're back!"

I sat up and looked at her shining face. "I know, honey. I woke up earlier and looked out the window."

She hugged me and then hurried to get dressed. By the time I had done so, she was outside, drinking in the beautiful morning. We used the shower house and I brought breakfast makings out to the picnic table. Dinah was reluctant to go back in the camper.

"Are we going home now?" she asked over a bite of cereal.

"As soon as we can pack things up." I was as anxious for this adventure to be over as she was.

"None of my friends are going to believe this."

"You're right, and that's why we shouldn't tell anyone. Seriously, they will think we're crazy. We'll both end up on the funny farm."

She put down a large gooey Danish I had bought at the bakery. I don't bake much.

"You're right. I'd think anyone was nuts who told me this."

I nodded. "Mum's the word."

She ate the rest of her breakfast in silence, and when we finished, I did the dishes while she packed up our lawn chairs, the tablecloth, and other outdoor stuff. She finally agreed to come back in and help get the camper ready for travel only because she was in such a hurry to get home.

Which we did by midmorning. Dinah was pretty quiet. She did help unload the trailer willingly, but then disappeared into her room. When I checked on her a half hour later, she was sound asleep on her bed, fully clothed. Good. Neither of us had rested well the night before and we had been under a lot of stress.

I didn't think I could sleep myself but fixed a glass of ice water and curled up in a lounge chair on my screened-in back porch. The book in my lap remained unopened. I could see the little trailer from where I sat. There was nothing menacing about it—nothing distinctive about it at all except quaintness. The whole weekend became more vague and unreal the longer I sat there.

I have known Ben Walker most of my life. There was no way I would believe that he knew about this and sold me the trailer without telling me that it might be a time machine or portal or whatever you call it. He simply wouldn't have sold it to me.

I must have dozed off, because the next thing I knew, Dinah was standing over me.

"Mom?"

"Yeah." I sat up and rubbed one eye with the heel of my hand.

"I'm going over to Tish's house."

"Oh. Um, do you want something to eat? What time is it?"

"It's after 2:00. I had a sandwich."

"Wow. I didn't think I would sleep. Be back by 6:00, okay?"

"Sure." She was out the door. It crossed my mind to remind her not to share anything about our weekend, but felt instinctively that wasn't going to be a problem. I drifted around the house aimlessly for about half an hour doing little odd jobs, and then decided that since Dinah was gone for the afternoon, I would start on that wallpaper. I knew that she didn't want anything more to do with the trailer but I still liked the office plan. The guesthouse idea would be a little shaky in the light of what we thought happened when you slept in it.

Armed with a spray bottle of vinegar water and a putty knife, I tackled the area around the couch. It was slow going; this paper was obviously made before the 'strippable' glues came out. By 5:30, I had only done the wall immediately above the couch. And, yes, it was all mint green underneath.

THE WEEK SEEMED long. I worked on the trailer in my spare time and Dinah kept to herself. I couldn't seem to draw her out. I suggested a movie or little shopping trip, but she declined, like she was afraid to even get in the car with me. The following weekend, Kurt picked her up again and I was on my own. I managed to get the rest of the wallpaper off and started ripping up the carpet. At least it would go a long way toward getting rid of the musty smell. Underneath was a faded linoleum — 1940s, I would guess.

I leaned back against the wall, my utility knife in hand. Both the wallpaper and the carpet appeared to be from the 1960s — about the time that Ben said he and his wife quit using it. We had gone back to the early 1960s. Maybe it was connected to the renovations.

On Sunday after church, I spotted Ben Walker at the coffee hour. I carried my coffee over to where he was sitting.

"Hey, travelin' lady! How's that camper doing? Have you been anywhere in it?"

I sat down next to him at the table. "Dinah and I took it out to Parson's Grove last weekend."

"Good!" He slapped the table lightly. "Everything work okay?"

"Yeah," I nodded and watched his face. There was no sign of duplicity there. "I've been taking the wallpaper and carpet out this week."

"Oh, gosh," he said and looked a little sad. "I put that in after Minnie died. But I never camped in it again after that."

"I'm sorry. It was in pretty bad shape…"

He covered my hand with his. "Of course! It just brings back memories, that's all."

"Under the paper is light green paint."

He laughed. "My mother did that—must have been in the early Fifties. My dad had a fit—covering all that wood up. But she had painted several rooms in the house that color and said all of that wood was too dark. I was just glad it wasn't pink."

We visited a little longer and I was satisfied that Ben knew nothing about the little trailer's other traveling abilities.

That afternoon, I finished tearing out the carpet and cleaned the trailer well. The paint would have to wait for another time.

CHAPTER TEN
Dinah

 DINAH CLIMBED THE steps of the library with some trepidation. She had been a frequent visitor in her younger years but not so much recently. She hoped her card was still good.

She had researched time travel on the Internet but the articles either talked about things like quantum physics or appeared to be written by nut cases who weren't grounded in the real world. Her mom was right; that's exactly how they would seem to anyone they tried to tell their tale to. Some of the articles mentioned fiction books that sounded more to her liking so she decided to see what she could find.

Inside the library was noisier than she remembered. A group of toddlers were gathered off to one side around a woman holding up a book to show them the pictures that went with a story. They tumbled over each other, hands raised in an effort to ask a question or share an experience. In a computer room visible through windows, people of all ages filled every station. A couple of older boys she had seen at school argued about something around a table in another corner.

She went to search the fiction stacks with the names of several books written on a scrap of paper. It was silly, she knew, but she was afraid if she asked the librarian for help, someone might guess what had happened to her.

She found Jack Finney's *Time and Again* and pulled it off the shelf.

"That's a good one. One of the classics."

She jumped and turned to see an old guy — probably twenty at least — watching her. She blushed, feeling both flustered at talking to an older guy and guilty that she had been found out.

"Have you read it?" she stammered.

"Yeah, I love science fiction and especially time travel. You, too?"

"Um — well, I just started — yeah."

"Have you read *The Time Machine*? That's one of the first ones written." He had unruly brown hair and piercing black eyes. Dinah hoped he wouldn't ask why she was interested.

"But that's a good one to start with." He nodded at the book in her hand when she didn't answer.

"Good. I think I'll take it." She fled to the circulation desk.

The man at the desk looked up her name on a computer, made a few clicks, and said, "We'll have to update your information and get your picture."

"My picture?" She was alarmed. Someone had tipped them off about her weekend.

"Yeah. We use pictures of all our patrons in our files now." He pulled out a small digital camera from under the desk.

"Oh." She stood frozen as he snapped her picture.

"Big Brother is watching you."

She jerked around to see the young man from the stacks standing right behind her.

"What?"

"*Nineteen-Eighty Four*. George Orwell," he said.

"Oh." She still didn't know what he meant, but grabbed her book. "Thanks."

Outside, she took a deep breath, relaxed a little and slipped the book into her backpack. Home was about five blocks away, which gave her plenty of time for worry and reflection. Her experiences of the weekend made her feel like an outsider at school. She still wasn't sure that the whole thing wasn't a bad dream. She and her mom hadn't talked about it. In a way, she wanted to put it behind her; in another it would help if Mom said something, just to confirm that they had the same experience, that Mom was as shaken by it as Dinah was.

But, no, yesterday when she got home from school, Mom had been out in that damn trailer, happily stripping the old Sixties wallpaper off the walls. When Dinah questioned her, she said she was going ahead with plans to make it an office.

Great idea. What if one of her clients got sucked back in time while he or she was in the midst of making plans to just go to China?

Dinah felt so alone.

OVER THE NEXT week, she devoured three of the books on her list. The older guy was in the library again when she checked out the third and asked her what she thought of *Time and Again*. She mumbled something stupid like "it was pretty good" and got away as fast as she could.

One of the things that didn't ring true in the books she was reading was how quickly the main characters accepted time travel. They were disbelieving at first but that didn't last long. It was like, "Oh yeah. Ho-hum. Here I go again. Big deal." She, however, found it harder and harder to accept. As time went on, she became more convinced it was a dream.

The only thing she knew for certain is that she wasn't sleeping in that thing again.

During the weekend, she had stayed with her dad. She decided to sound him out over pizza.

"Dad, have you ever read any books about time travel?"

He thought about it. "I don't think so. I'm not much into sci-fi. Wait—I guess I had to read *The Time Machine* in high school but I don't remember much about it."

She told him what she was reading and asked him if he thought time travel was possible.

"I doubt it. There's all of those questions, you know, about whether you could meet yourself at a younger age or kill your grandfather." He grinned at her.

"Kill your grandfather? Why would you want to do that?"

"It's just a hypothetical about whether you *could*. If you go back and change history, what does that do to the present?"

"It's very confusing," she said, and changed the subject.

CHAPTER ELEVEN

A WEEK OR SO after we got back from Parsons' Grove (and points beyond), my mother invited Dinah and me over for supper. I must admit, I am a little jealous of my mother. All of the smiles, jokes, and confidences that I wish Dinah would share with me, she gives to my mother. Apparently, grandmothers can do no wrong.

"I haven't seen you in weeks!" Mom said, giving Dinah a big hug and exaggerating a little. "How's school?"

"We have a chorus concert next week, Gram—can you come?"

Huh. I hadn't been informed about this yet. See what I mean?

"Of course," Mom said. "Day and time?"

"Tuesday at 7:00."

"I'll be there." Mom high-fived Dinah, who actually responded. I would have received an eye-roll.

We sat down to pork chops, potatoes, gravy and fresh asparagus. Mom quizzed Dinah about what numbers the chorus would be performing and then turned to me.

"Did you ever decide what color you're going to paint the kitchen?" She has an understandable interest in everything I do to my house. She had lived there until my marriage to Kurt fifteen years ago. She and Dad sold us the house and bought the very small Craftsman bungalow that she lived in now. Dad passed away suddenly a year after they moved.

"I'm thinking of kind of a celery green."

"Nooo," Dinah whined. "Purple! Let's paint it purple."

I made a 'wrong answer' sound and she turned to her grandmother. "Gram, so—you've only lived in two houses your whole life?"

"That's right—well, except when I was in college and a couple of years when my dad was transferred to Nebraska."

That caught my attention. "Nebraska?"

"Sure. He sold grain bins you know, and the company sent him out there to start a new territory. I was in fourth grade. We moved back when I was ready to start sixth grade."

About ten years old, I thought. "So how did you end up with the same house?" Dinah said.

"We just rented it while we were gone."

Was Dinah just curious or looking for an explanation for the strange man we had seen leaving the house back in 1962? She didn't look at me so I wasn't sure.

But the real shock was still to come. "Mom," I said, "did you ever know Ben Walker's wife Minnie?"

She shook her head. "Ben was never married. Not that I knew anyway. Ben is ten or fifteen years older than me. I do remember hearing that he was madly in love with someone before he moved here but she ran off with another guy."

I realized I was sitting with my mouth open. "But he's told me about Minnie several times...and all the fun they had camping in that trailer I bought from him."

"No, Minnie may have been the name of the girl, but I'm sure they never were married. He's always been single since I've known him."

THE NEXT WEEKEND, Dinah would be going to Kurt's again. It was usually every other weekend but he had asked to trade because he had a business trip on his next regular weekend.

Dinah showed no signs of ever wanting to camp again or talk about our weekend. I didn't want to push her. But my curiosity was growing about the trailer. Was our trip a freak thing or a figment of our imagination?

I knew I didn't want to expose Dinah to a repeat experience, but I was dying to know whether it would happen again. I went on line and found another county park with camping about forty miles away. I wanted to stick with places with fewer people. For one thing, if this was really happening, I still wondered if the trailer and car disappeared from the present. Didn't that cause people to wonder why it was gone Saturday morning and back Sunday morning? It could be explained but still might cause questions and I wanted to avoid those whenever possible. The park and the campground dated back to the 1930s so I thought that was safe. I didn't want to go back in time and end up in a cattle yard.

So after Kurt picked Dinah up on Friday, I hurried to load some basic supplies and a few clothes. I stuck with jeans and plain shirts that wouldn't seem too out of place for quite a few decades back. If I went back farther than that I would be in trouble. Maybe I'd have to pull a Scarlett O'Hara and tear down the curtains to make an appropriate outfit. However, given the length of the curtains, about all I could make would be a showgirl's costume. I hoped it wouldn't come to that. Besides, I don't know how to sew. As an afterthought, I searched the box of jewelry that Dinah had found. I selected a charm bracelet, heavy with baubles and fastened it around my wrist.

With a few do-overs, I managed to get the car backed up and the trailer hitched. I sat in the car for a minute looking at the map to make sure I knew where I was going and then set off.

It was a gray spring evening. The leaves on the trees had gone from wispy lime green to fuller clumps of leaves. Spotty rain was predicted but I had a couple of books along that were almost overdue at the library. When I arrived at the campground, I was delighted to see that there were still some empty sites along the shore of the small lake. I took the end one, which was partly shielded from the rest of the campground by a little ravine and a thicket of trees. I could park my car at an angle so the license plates wouldn't be obvious and the only one on the trailer would be toward the lake.

I managed to get the trailer backed in with less toing-and-froing than my previous attempts. I was getting good. That's my story and I'm sticking to it.

Once I was set up, I made a cold meat loaf sandwich with ketchup—one of the world's great delicacies in my mind—and took my supper and my book out to the picnic table. It was right down by the water and gave me a view along the lake shore to a little sandy beach where a youngish woman sat watching two toddlers fill buckets with sand and pour them out. The sun descended and produced a soft yellow glow across the western sky.

I closed my book for want of a reading light and briefly wished I had my ereader, which for obvious reasons, I had left at home. But I stayed at my spot until full dark, watching the stars come out. It was not too late to change my mind. I could hook the trailer back up, head home, and spend the night in my safe little bed.

But I had by this time convinced myself that the time travel weekend was nothing more than what Dinah said at the time—a nightmare. If I stayed in the trailer this weekend, and nothing happened, I could put it out of my mind.

So with most of me hoping I would wake up in the present—and only a very small part curious about the past—I went to bed.

CHAPTER TWELVE
Dinah

DINAH PULLED A book from the shelf and flipped the cover open to read the flyleaf. She hadn't heard of this one but thought it looked interesting. She picked out a couple of others and pushed open the side door of the library to a patio furnished with tables, chairs and umbrellas. A pushcart to one side sold coffee and a small selection of scones and muffins. She chose a banana muffin to go with her black coffee and took them to an empty table away from the other patrons.

It was a beautiful Saturday morning, even though rain had been forecast. She munched the muffin and began to read the first chapter of the top book on her stack.

"Hi! We meet again."

She looked up and saw with dismay the same young man she had encountered twice before.

"Are you following me?"

"What? Oh, no—I didn't mean to scare you. My name's Bret, by the way, and I just spend a lot of time here at the library. Can I join you?"

Dinah looked around. People filled several other tables plus the woman who presided over the pushcart. Seemed safe enough.

"I guess."

He pulled out a chair and set down his coffee. "What do you have there?"

"A couple that I hadn't heard of. I was just seeing if I thought I would like them."

He picked up one. "Hmm. That's a new one on me, too. What else have you read?"

"I just finished *The House on the Strand*. I forget who wrote it."

"Daphne du Maurier," he said.

"Yeah." She decided to take a risk and ask him a couple of questions. "It doesn't seem like they explain much about how the time travel occurs. I mean, in that one it was drugs, and sometimes it's hypnosis. Or there's a machine built for that purpose. Does anybody ever think it just happens, like at a certain place or anything? I mean, I know none of it's true..."

He raised one eyebrow. "Isn't it?"

She blushed. "No!"

He backed off. "It interests me," he explained, "because we calculate time down to the nth degree but it's still subjective. How it feels—think of the words we use: time drags, time flies, time stands still, and so on. Why do we have so many conflicting phrases to describe it if it's so exact? Feelings of deja vu bring up other questions—it just makes me wonder if there isn't a way to cross over. Of course, I know nothing for sure."

She nodded and didn't know what to say.

"Stephen King put a time portal in an old diner in *11/22/63* like you're talking about." He wrote down a couple of other titles for her.

She piled up her books and crushed her coffee cup. "I'd better be going. My dad expects me back soon." He didn't but Dinah still felt uncomfortable around Bret. "Thanks for the suggestions. I'll see you around."

CHAPTER THIRTEEN

IT WAS STILL dark when I woke the next morning. It took a couple of minutes to orient myself and realize the possibilities. I may look out the window and see the same scene I had enjoyed the night before, the same campers of varying sizes and ages scattered around the campground, the same trees and shrubs. On the other hand, I may see the same locale at a different time—two or three decades earlier, maybe even centuries earlier. I hadn't thought of that before. What if I was in prehistoric times? Shades of Jurassic Park.

What if I didn't get up and look? What if I lay here all day and hoped sleep would bring me back from wherever I might be? Okay, not so practical. For one thing, I would need to go to the bathroom. And I knew going all day without eating really was beyond my willpower.

At the least, I could lay here until light. That seemed less threatening. I would do that.

I thought about Christmas mornings as a kid. The difference was that on those mornings I was pretty sure of a positive outcome. Santa might not leave me exactly what I wanted but I wasn't worried about total losers.

However, the longer I stayed in bed, the more disastrous scenarios I could come up with. So I pushed myself up and pulled back the curtain in the corner window. Gray light was just beginning to come across the lake. Enough to see that the thicket of trees obscuring my campsite from the rest of the campground was not there.

After dressing, I cautiously opened the door. The gravel that I parked my camper on the night before was not there either—just dirt. Gone also were the trailers and motorhomes, and in their places, more tents and a few small 'vintage' trailers—although, if I was guessing right, probably not considered vintage by the owners.

The beach seemed larger. I could barely make out a sign at the edge of the beach by the campground road. Perhaps it would give me a clue.

I didn't see any people out so I walked toward the sign. At least I didn't have to worry about dinosaurs. The sign read: "Beach Closed to Prevent the Spread of Polio."

So it must be before 1955 and the Salk vaccine. I meant to study up on vintage campers when I was home so that I would better be able to identify the year and hadn't done it. A little farther on, a stone bathhouse held a real plus—flush toilets. As I returned to my trailer, I was so thankful that I hadn't tried to coax Dinah into coming with me.

"Hi! Nice morning!"

I jumped a little at the voice, so lost in thought was I. I glanced over at a tent I was passing to see a woman sitting in a canvas chair by a small campfire leafing through a magazine. She was pretty and had auburn hair cut in a close-fitting cap with a couple of curls arranged around the face. She wore a tailored print blouse, open at the neck, with knee length pants and a small scarf tied around her neck.

"Yes, it is," I replied.

"Is that your camper?" She nodded toward the trailer and got up to walk over to me.

"Yes."

"How old is it?"

"1937. It was my grandfather's."

"That's something!" she said. "Can I peek inside?"

I tried to remember if any thing questionable was out. "Sure," I said, crossing my fingers. I went in first and held the door for her,

"Oh, what a great color! That makes it look so much more modern. Did you do that?"

"Um, sort of."

Too late, I noticed my book on the dinette right before she did — a book that wouldn't be a best seller for another fifty or sixty years.

"What are you reading?" She picked it up and examined the cover. "I've never heard of this writer."

I thought fast, for once. "I'm a book editor. That's an advance copy — it isn't out yet. A new writer." I took it from her gently so she wouldn't turn it over and see how many books the author had actually written. "I'm not supposed to let anyone see it," I added, winking at her.

She put her hand over her mouth. "Oh, sorry. So you're not from around here."

"No," I said and left it at that.

"Where's your husband?" she asked, looking around for masculine paraphernalia.

"I'm not married," I said as I opened the door and went back outside, hoping she would take the hint. She did.

"Really?" Lord, this woman was chatty. "Who pulls your camper?"

"I do."

"You're kidding."

"No." Why didn't I just say my husband was gone for the day?

"Well, that's—wonderful. I'd better get going. My name is Audrey, by the way."

"I'm Lynne. It's been nice talking to you." I watched her walk back to her campsite and went back in my own trailer. I collapsed at the dinette. Travel may be broadening but time travel was exhausting.

I needed to get my story straight before any more questions. I wasn't sure which would be less acceptable in the early Fifties (which I assumed I was in); being divorced or being in my late thirties and never having been married.

I fixed a bowl of cereal to have with a muffin and poured another cup of coffee. While I ate, I watched out the dinette window as more people began to stir around the campground. During the last trip, I had avoided people as much as possible. This time, I wanted to interact a little more but on a limited basis. I decided to go the never married route. It would probably evoke more sympathy than disapproval.

I ventured out again after taking care of my dishes, wishing I had a dog to walk as an excuse for perusing the campground. I dumped my garbage out of the ubiquitous 21st century plastic bag into a brown paper sack. As I walked, I looked at first for a dumpster but realized it would probably be a trash barrel or metal garbage can.

A barrel stood near the bathhouse and just as I threw in my sack, a man about my age dressed in gray slacks and a short sleeved white sport shirt, both pressed to an amazing crispness, walked up with a folded newspaper. He was about to pitch it in so I drew my gaze away from the ironing job and said, "Is that today's paper?"

"Yes — do you want it?"

I held out my hand. "If you wouldn't mind. I haven't been anywhere to pick one up this morning."

"Say, you just enjoy it, little lady." He handed it to me and took a cigarette out of his shirt pocket. As he lit it with a large silver lighter, he glanced sideways at me and winked. The epithet and the wink rankled in away that Ben Walker calling me 'young lady' never did, but I wasn't here to make waves so I thanked him and walked back to my trailer. I tried to carry the paper casually without even sneaking a peek at the date to give anyone watching the impression that it was just a welcome little diversion rather than containing information that I desperately needed to ground me in the 'present.'

Once back at my dinette, I impatiently spread the paper out on the wooden table. It was a daily paper and the date in the masthead said May 22, 1954.

I scanned the headlines but before I read any of the stories, a couple of notices caught my eye. A small box near the bottom tallied the polio deaths for the year. That number hit me harder than even the sign on the beach. Another larger box summarized the major stories for the week. On Monday, the Supreme Court had handed down their landmark decision in *Brown v. The Board of Education of Topeka, Kansas*. There were other follow-up stories about the French loss of Dien Bien Phu in Vietnam and Roger Bannister's four-minute mile—only a couple of weeks in the past.

I had learned about these events in my history classes but it was totally different to think of them as current happenings. The people living them didn't know how they were going to turn out, what effect on their lives they were going to have. I thought about the end of the polio epidemic in the next few years; the end of parents' fear every summer to let their kids swim or hang out with their friends. I thought also about the civil rights turmoil facing the country in the next decades and the vast changes to society that would result from the Viet Nam War. I thought I really would not like to live through those years knowing what was coming.

CHAPTER FOURTEEN

 I SPENT MORE than an hour reading that paper, trying to get as much of a handle on my new 'present' as I could. It was getting warm in the trailer so I decided on some beach time.

There was a young mother with a small child wielding a pail and shovel at one end. Three pre-teen boys chased each other in circles, throwing buckets of water. A young woman sat alone staring at the lake, arms around her knees. As I got closer, I noticed that she looked like she'd been crying.

"Are you okay?" I asked her.

She glanced up at me. Short dark curls framed a porcelain complexion and bright blue eyes.

"Yeah. Men!" she said and shook her head. She sighed and slumped her shoulders.

I sat down in the sand near her. "I know. You can't live with 'em and you can't live without 'em." Very clever and original. But she must not have heard it before because she giggled a little.

"Are you camping here?" I asked.

She shook her head. "I just came out for a little time alone."

"Oh, I'm sorry." I started to get up.

"No, no," she said. "I just wanted to get away from my mother for a while. She means well, but she drives me crazy."

"That happens," I said.

"She forgets this is modern times, not the Twenties or Thirties. She's always trying to give me advice."

"Like you said, I'm sure she means well."

"She didn't like my boyfriend and now he broke up with me."

"But your mom didn't have anything to do with that, did she?"

She didn't say anything for a few minutes.

"My boyfriend was in Korea for a year and a half. We were going to be married when he got home and now he broke up with me. She told him I was going out with someone else." Tears started again.

"Did you?" I asked, curious.

"No. I mean, I went out a couple of times with another guy, and he was pretty serious, but I never was. Sorry to put all of this on you."

"Don't worry. I'll never tell a soul, but sometimes it helps to talk about it." I ran my fingers through the sand. "So what are you going to do?"

She shrugged. "Nothing I can do. My boyfriend—I guess he's not my boyfriend any more—says it's definitely over."

"It might be difficult to ever build back trust if he feels like that," I said, conscious that I shouldn't be giving any advice that could change history.

"I know." She noticed the bracelet on my wrist. "That looks heavy." She watched my face carefully, perhaps wondering if she had offended me.

"It is," I admitted.

She stood up and brushed the sand off her jeans. "I'd better get to work. Thanks for listening." She gave me a little smile and walked away.

I stayed on the beach for a while. The rhythm of the waves on sand was soothing and relaxing. When I looked around the campground, life appeared more peaceful and less complicated than my own time, but I knew from the newspaper that was only on the surface.

By the time I returned to my trailer, I felt I could justify lunch. I spent the afternoon reading inside, not wanting to press my luck in the interaction department. However, I can only stay inside so long and I needed a trip to the bathroom so late afternoon, out I went. There was a lot of activity, with several campfires lending smoke to the air, and I nodded at people working on their suppers as I passed.

I received a few stares, but more in the nature of trying to figure out if they knew me rather than of the "I wonder if she comes from the future" type. My supper was as simple as the rest of my meals—a leftover dish of casserole I had brought from home and a bowl of fruit. I did decide to start a small fire and sit outside after supper. I was reading more of the paper at the picnic table when Audrey and the man who had given it to me walked by hand-in-hand. He stopped and pulled his wife (I assume) into my campsite.

"That's quite a camper you have there," he said.

"Thanks," I said, taking it as a compliment.

"My wife says you pull it yourself?"

"Yes."

"How do you back it up?" he asked, and I wanted to answer "How does anyone?" but thought better of it.

"Not very well, but I get the job done."

He snickered and pointed at me. "You need to get yourself a man, missy."

"Harry!" Audrey said, and slapped him playfully on the arm. Her little smile said that she was certainly glad that she wasn't in my predicament.

Harry sat down across from me and pulled Audrey down beside him. He lit up a cigarette.

"Audrey says you're a book editor?" Audrey must have given him a very full report.

"Yes, I am."

"Just what do you do as an 'editor'?"

"I look at a lot of manuscripts that writers are hoping to publish, and work with a couple of writers who are under contract."

He smirked. "I 'spose you run into a few Commie writers in that job."

"What?"

"You know, we watched those McCarthy hearings on television and it seems like a lot of the Reds in this country are actors or musicians or writers. I imagine you have to weed those out." He looked at me intently, daring me to disagree.

"I handle mostly fiction."

"Still…"

"Harry, don't be so nosy." Audrey tapped his arm again. The rebuke was gentle and ladylike. She turned to me. "Harry's favorite TV show is *I Led Three Lives*."

"I'm not nosy. Every citizen in this great country has to be watchful." He turned back to me. "You had to take a loyalty oath on your job, didn't you?"

A what? "Um, yes I did." Seemed to be the right answer.

"There you go!" He sat back and slapped the table. "You can't even be too careful about fiction. We cleaned a bunch of books out of our local library, including all of that guy Steinbeck's trash." He got up and motioned Audrey to join him. "Gotta go finish our walk. I have some friends dropping by later."

As they walked on down the road, Harry chattered away, bending down to say something occasionally in Audrey's ear and glancing back at me. I felt dirty, like I had been judged, and the verdict wasn't good. When they returned to their campsite, Audrey kissed her husband and went into the tent and he sat by his fire. It was full dark now and I decided it was time for me to turn in too.

Harry and his attitude made me nervous. I heard cars pull in. When I peeked out between the curtains, I could that see a couple of men had joined Harry and at one point he pointed over at my trailer. I quickly closed the curtains and doused the lights. Perhaps Harry was telling his friends admiringly what a woman I was to pull my own trailer, but more likely he was pointing me out as a threat to national security.

I slipped off the charm bracelet and crawled into bed and, while I waited for the Thought Police to bang on my door, I fervently hoped the trailer worked the same way as last time.

Chapter Fifteen

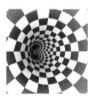 I WAS SURPRISED when I woke up that it was light and I had slept heavily through the night. This time I jumped out of bed to look outside. The trailers and motorhomes that had been there when I went to bed Friday night were back. I collapsed on my couch/bed and leaned against the wall in relief. After a moment, I felt sufficiently collected to fix my coffee.

I pulled my phone out of the pocket of my jacket hanging on a wall hook and was delighted when the screen lit up. Yesterday it had been black. Oh, oh—a missed call from Dinah. I was pretty sure she wasn't up yet; I would give her a call later.

I took my coffee outside and noted that across the road Harry, Audrey, their tent, and their friends were gone. A big relief—no worry about being hauled in before the House Un-American Activities Committee. Puddles around my site and on the road testified to rain sometime in the last twenty-four hours.

An hour later, breakfast finished and things packed up in the trailer, I sat down to call Dinah. She answered immediately.

"Mom!" It wasn't a question but rather an accusation. "Where are you? You took the trailer again!"

I resisted reacting like a chastened child although that's the way I felt. "It's my trailer," I said.

"I know." Now the worry came through in her voice. "Where did you take it? What happened? Are you okay?"

I took a deep breath. "I'm fine. For now, let's just say it was similar to the last trip. I'm getting ready to head home—I should be there in an hour and a half." It was time to talk this out with Dinah. Her memories were obviously similar to mine, or she wouldn't be so worried.

A LITTLE OVER an hour later, I was back home. I got the trailer parked and headed for the house with my laundry bag. Dinah sat on the steps waiting.

"Oh!" I said. "Couldn't you get in?'

"Yeah, I already took my stuff in. I was just waiting for you." She gave me a hug.

"Let's go inside." I dropped my laundry bag at the top of the basement stairs and went into the dining room. Dinah had placed two steaming mugs on the table.

"I made coffee," she said. "Don't look so surprised—I'm fourteen."

Which usually means that you refuse to do anything constructive, I thought, but instead said, "It'll stunt your growth."

"Least of my worries." She sat by one of the mugs and wrapped her hands around it. "Tell me what's going on. I had just convinced myself that our camping trip was a dream."

"I thought so too, but it happened again." I told her about my weekend and the people I met. Her eyes widened when I got to the part about Harry and the loyalty oath stuff.

"Were you still in America?"

"Oh, yes. People were so concerned about nuclear war and the power of the Soviet Union that they saw spies behind every bush."

"Like the kid hunting for Russians the time before. Wow."

"Wow is right. You can imagine how relieved I was to wake up this morning in 2014, and also how glad I was you weren't with me."

I expected an argument about that but she surprised me. "Well, if I had been along, you probably wouldn't have gotten much sympathy for never having been married."

"You're right."

She asked the same question I'd been asking myself. "Do you think Ben knows about this?"

"I've wondered, but I don't think he would have sold it to me if he did. But what Grandma Linda told us about him never having been married concerns me too. Maybe he's losing his memory."

"I've been reading a lot of time travel books. Do you think that might make people suspicious?"

"Think about it, honey. If you had a friend who read fantasy books about space, would you suspect them of harboring an alien somewhere?"

"Now? Or before our first camping trip?"

"Before."

"No, I see what you mean. But in most of the books, people are trying to go back in time. But we didn't. We just kind of slipped—"

"Down the rabbit hole?" I finished for her. *Alice in Wonderland* had been one of her favorite books and movies when she was little.

"Yeah."

"Here's my theory. Each time I remove some of the 'remodeling,' it takes it back to the time the previous addition was made. I replaced the cushions. Before those cushions were made, around 1962, Ben says his wife had just put up the wallpaper and had the carpet installed. I took out the wallpaper and the carpet and it took me back to 1954, about when Ben's mother painted it green."

She stared at me in silence for a moment. "That's got to be it. What if we take the paint off?"

"Then it would go back to either when something else was done or when it was new. I don't know if anything else might have been done to it."

"What about the jewelry? You thought that bracelet might have had something to do with it."

"And it might. I had a 50s charm bracelet on during the last trip. But I didn't wear it last night when I wanted to come back."

"That might just be coincidence."

"It could be. But I wasn't going to wear it another night and take a chance on Harry and his cronies carting me off."

The phone rang. It was my mother.

"Lynne! I didn't know if you had heard. Ben Walker had a stroke last night. He's in the hospital."

"Oh, no!" I was doubly dismayed. First, for Ben's health and the fact that he has no immediate family that I know of. Second, that I was ready to ask him some direct questions about the trailer, but that wouldn't be a good idea for a while.

Mom gave me the information about the hospital and what else she knew, which wasn't much. I hung up and told Dinah.

"I'll need to go visit him. I'd planned to sound him out more about the trailer but that will have to wait. Poor guy. Wish I knew the story about his 'marriage.' Well, I'm going to finish unloading the trailer, shower, and then go and see how he's doing."

"I'll go with you," Dinah said.

"That would be great," I said, happy to have her focusing on someone outside herself.

CHAPTER SIXTEEN

WE GOT DIRECTIONS from the Patient Information desk and were just arriving as Patsy Bergen, our minister, was leaving.

"Hey, Pastor Patsy," Dinah said.

"Hey, Dinah, Lynne."

"How's Ben?" I said.

Patsy looked worried, and she glanced back toward the room. "I don't know. He's not awake and they have him hooked up to every machine in the place, I think."

"We won't stay long," I said. "See you later."

Patsy gave a thumbs up sign and headed down the hall.

The area around Ben's bed was darkened and he lay perfectly still. Tubes snaked out of his arms and chest and machines hummed a lullaby of sorts.

Dinah and I stood silently for a few minutes watching him when a nurse walked in with a clipboard.

"How's he doing?" I said.

She tipped her head and looked at me over her glasses. "You family?"

"No, just good friends." I wondered what her reaction would be if I added, 'We're the ones who bought his time-traveling trailer.' But I just said, "I don't think he has any family."

She checked her clipboard. "Ehh—there's a sister on the West Coast but not able to travel."

"So there's no one here you can give his condition to?"

"We're still checking." She swished out of the room.

We followed her out.

As we headed for the car, Dinah said, "Are you going to try it again?"

"The camper?"

"Yeah."

"I don't know. We've been lucky so far, but since we don't know how it works..."

"I want to do it again." Her eyes were bright as she searched my face for my response.

I shook my head. "Why?"

"Because the first time, I was so scared, I don't really feel like I experienced any of it."

"Dinah, I just said that just because it's worked twice doesn't mean..."

She interrupted. "Just because we've never had an accident going to Grandma's for supper or to church doesn't mean it can't happen."

"That's different..."

"How? There's a risk, but there's always a risk. And what's the worst thing that can happen? We get stuck in the 'good old days?'"

I gave her a sharp look. "You'd be okay with that?"

"Not okay, but we'd still be alive."

Who can argue with fourteen-year-old logic? "We don't know for sure where or when we'd end up…"

"But you have it figured out."

"No, I don't…just a theory. I don't know, Dinah, I have to think about it."

We'd reached the car and got in, with Dinah slamming her door harder than necessary. She pulled out her phone and began texting. After several back and forths, she said, "Can I go to the movie tonight with Tish?"

"In town?"

"Yeah."

"Okay."

The local theater only showed PG movies, was cheap, and early enough for a school night. We rode the rest of the way home in silence. I was very torn about Dinah's desire to try the trailer again. Another *Be careful what you wish for* moment. The evening would give me time to think about it more carefully.

She spent the afternoon curled up with one of her time travel novels on the back porch. Was she accepting everything she read as gospel truth? I worried that our experiences plus the fantasies she read would loosen her hold on reality. After that thought, I was immediately glad I hadn't made *that* statement in an NPR interview or something. Our experiences had no hold on reality.

When we sat down to a light supper before she went to the movie, I said, "We both need to remember that the books you're reading are fiction."

"As far as we know," she said.

"Yes, as far as we know. So they certainly aren't research in the usual sense. But in any of them, do people go back in time unintentionally?"

She thought a moment. "A couple. But most of them take some kind of action to make the change."

"Like what?"

"Oh, hypnosis or a gadget like a belt."

"Well, I still want to consider another trip very carefully. And be better prepared. Tomorrow, after we get home, we're going to do a little shopping."

"Where?" She was suspicious.

"I think Second Hand Violet's and Just Junk."

"Oh, I get it." She allowed a little smile to slip out. Violet's sold vintage clothing and Just Junk was exactly that.

"What are you looking for at Junk's?" she asked.

"I've seen old license plates there, for one thing."

THE NEXT DAY I hurried home after work and found Dinah already waiting for me. As we drove to Violet's she said, "How do you know what era to buy?"

"The older the better. I have clothes that are eight or ten years old."

"I know." She grimaced.

"They're not that bad. Anyway, we can get by with things from earlier years that are just out of style; it's the stuff from the future we need to be careful of."

"The future?"

"I mean, ahead of the time we're in. Like Fifties clothes in the Forties. Thirties clothes in the Fifties would be less of a problem."

In the store, we wiggled through close-set racks of clothes. Dinah spotted something she liked on every rack but had the good sense for once to realize this was not the time. Literally.

I found a rack of dresses and blouses from the 1930s and motioned Dinah over.

"Dresses?" was all she could say.

"I know, but pants and shorts were only starting to appear. Try these on." I handed her three cotton print dresses on hangers. One even had an embroidered hankie pinned to one shoulder.

She stood holding them with disgust and pointed to the hankie. "What's this?"

I explained and she frowned. "You mean somebody might have blown their nose on this?"

"I'm sure they did. Relax—it's been washed. Go try them on."

A gigantic eye-roll and off she went to a small closet with a curtain that served as a dressing room. I had gathered several things for myself and laid them on a chair by the dressing room when she came out wearing a blue-checked dress with short sleeves, a white collar, and slightly flared skirt. It was not the one with the hankie. My first thought on seeing her was of Judy Garland in *The Wizard of Oz*. She just needed white anklets and a pair of Mary Janes.

"Perfect," I said, ready to combat any argument she presented, when she caught sight of herself in the mirror.

"Hey! Not bad. I could be in a play or something. It doesn't look like me."

I laughed. "Certainly not like the you I see most of the time. It's a little long but I need to pack needles and thread. If we end up in the Forties, I could shorten it. Skirts got shorter during the war."

Dinah smirked. "A treat for the boys going off to battle?"

"No, a shortage of fabric. Try on one of the others and I'll find you a pair of shorts."

"Great," she said, ducking behind the curtain. It was not a vote of confidence.

I found a tailored white short-sleeved blouse and pink slightly flared shorts. When she tried them on, she pulled at the high waist and wide legs of the shorts, giving me an almost pleading look.

"You said you could be in a play. If we do this, that's what we have to pretend—that we are someone else living in a different time." I glanced around to make sure no one was listening.

She nodded. "Okay. Now you try yours on." I did, each one critiqued at first with giggles and snorts but then a more serious thumbs up or thumbs down. We chose two cotton print house dresses and a pair of slacks with a plain black blouse for me.

"What about shoes?" Dinah said.

"I think we can get by. I've got a pair of wedge sandals kind of like those," I pointed at a pair of tan shoes, "and you have those saddle shoes that you wore for show choir."

I paid for our purchases and we headed for Just Junk in the same mini-mall. Here I had to control myself. We first picked out several sets of license plates from the 30s, 40s, and 50s. Despite my worries on the last trip about dinosaurs, I felt instinctively that the trailer could not go back earlier than its date of manufacture.

Then we wandered through the housewares. Dinah spotted a red-and-once-white metal breadbox and I found a pair of salt and pepper shakers and matching napkin holder. Did they use paper napkins in the Thirties? I'd have to check. We also picked up a set of metal camping pans and dishes that all fit inside one another.

"Mom!" Dinah called from a couple of aisles over. "Come check this out!"

She'd found a small tan radio of a plastic-like material with a square dial. A scrap of notebook paper had been taped to it, bearing the simple message: "Works!"

"You know, that's a great idea." I looked around to see if anyone was nearby. "It would be a way to find out the date, maybe."

We also picked up a couple of magazines as a hairstyle reference. By then, my meager bank account was depleted enough and I decided to call it quits for the day.

CHAPTER SEVENTEEN
Dinah

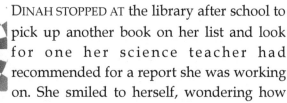 DINAH STOPPED AT the library after school to pick up another book on her list and look for one her science teacher had recommended for a report she was working on. She smiled to herself, wondering how Mrs. Patten would react if she changed her report topic to time travel instead of coral reefs. That was still science, right? Something had to explain it.

She found the novel and was headed to the science section when she passed Bret working at a table.

"Hey! Haven't seen you in a while. How's your reading coming?"

She smiled, more relaxed now around him. He seemed only interested in her reading habits. "I just finished *The Time Machine* and now I'm going to try this one." She held out the book for him to see.

He nodded approval at her choice. "What did you think of *Time Machine*?"

She sat down in an empty chair next to him. "It was cool."

"What do you think happened to him at the end? Where did he go?"

She thought a minute. "I think he went to the future but not so far ahead. I think he wanted to know how it all came about."

"Do you think he ever came back?"

"He might not want to," she said. "I mean, if he went ahead a hundred years or so, maybe he would want to see where all the scientific inventions and stuff would lead next."

"Or maybe he couldn't come back," Bret said.

"Oh. Does that ever happen? I mean, in the books you've read?" She paled a little.

"Sometimes. Not often. Because the interesting thing about these stories is the interaction between two time periods. So the writer usually makes them come back."

She nodded and chewed her lip a little. "I'd better go." She got up. "I have a report to do for school. See you around."

He smiled up at her. "Good luck on your report."

After she found the book she needed for her report, she went to the desk to check it out. The head librarian, Miss Swanson, was on duty. She was a friend of Grandma Linda's and about the same age.

"Hello, Dinah. Did you find what you were looking for?"

"Yeah, I just need to check these out."

While Miss Swanson looked up her account on the computer, she said in a lower voice, "You know Dinah, Bret seems to be a nice young man, but he is quite a bit older than you."

Dinah was so surprised that she forgot her manners and said, "So?"

"I'm just saying it's best not to get *too* friendly."

Dinah grabbed her books. "Thank you for your advice." She rushed out of the library before Miss Swanson saw the tears in her eyes.

CHAPTER EIGHTEEN

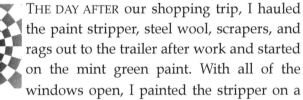THE DAY AFTER our shopping trip, I hauled the paint stripper, steel wool, scrapers, and rags out to the trailer after work and started on the mint green paint. With all of the windows open, I painted the stripper on a section of wall about a foot square. While I let it work, I examined all of the cubby holes and compartments again, hoping to discover more about the trailer's past. My only find was an aged brochure for the Black Hills.

After the paint bubbled up, I gently scraped it off and into an old coffee can. Underneath, the wood was the same warm brown finish as the cabinets. Eagerly, I cleaned the area with a little steel wool dipped in the stripper. It was going to be a long process but I was satisfied that the results would be worth it.

I closed things up and went in to make supper. Dinah had gone to the library again after school. I knew Dinah had been reading a lot of time travel novels, but all the same I hoped 'the library' wasn't a euphemism for some other less wholesome activity. Perhaps it was my imagination, but she did seem a little flustered and guilty-acting when she came in.

"What's for supper?" She slung her backpack on the kitchen counter where I've asked her not to leave it. At my look, she sighed, picked it up and dropped it in the dining room.

"I thought we'd go wild and crazy with hamburgers and coleslaw."

She shrugged, almost if she didn't hear me, and headed to her room. "Take your back pack with you," I called after her.

I could hear muttering as she went up the stairs and didn't want to know what it was about.

At supper, I told her I was going to go see how Ben was doing.

"I'd better stay here. I need to work on my science report."

"Okay. What's it about?"

"Coral reefs."

I left her to it after supper and drove to the hospital. There always seems to be a kind of a subdued busyness in hospitals at night. A woman I knew slightly from school functions manned the nurses' station.

"I'm here to see Ben Walker."

She grabbed a clipboard and scanned it. "He's in room 216. He's doing better today." She smiled at me.

"Good."

I was relieved to find Ben awake and sitting up, but he was still plugged in to various monitors.

"Hello, young lady!" he said with a feeble grin.

I gave him a kiss on the forehead and squeezed his right hand. His left arm appeared stiff and awkward.

"How are you doing? Dinah and I were here Sunday but you weren't your usual chatty self."

He sighed. "Stroke. As they say, getting old isn't for the faint of heart. Can't move my left arm."

"What are the doctors saying? They wouldn't tell us anything."

He shifted slightly in bed. "Tomorrow I'm going to the rehab facility — physical therapy for my arm."

"Well, that's a move up, right?"

"I guess. Could I ask you for a favor?"

"Sure. Anything."

"I need some clothes and stuff from the house. The key is under the gnome by the back door."

I smiled. "No one will ever look for it there, right?"

He shrugged. "I don't usually lock it myself. One of the paramedics told me they did it."

I took out a notepad and made a list of the items he needed.

"Thanks," he said. "I was going to ask Pastor Patsy but you got here first. It's hell being so helpless. So, are you busy at work?"

"It's picking up — people making last minute vacation plans."

"Have you been camping again?" I could swear there was a twinkle in his eye.

"Last weekend. Dinah spent the weekend with Kurt so I went by myself."

"Run into any rain?"

"Not there," I said and hoped he would ask where — or when — 'there' was. He didn't.

"I started stripping the green paint off the walls. I think it's going to turn out well."

"Good," he said, and then a sad look crossed his face. "Getting kind of sleepy, young lady."

"You rest. I need to go anyway. I'll get these things after work tomorrow if that's okay and bring them to you at the rehab center."

"That'll be fine." He was almost dozing so I squeezed his hand.

"Take care, Ben," I said and left.

THE NEXT DAY I closed my office a little early and drove out to Ben's farm. I brought along a couple of shopping bags to collect his stuff. The house was quiet and seemed eerily so, maybe because I was there and the owner wasn't. The decor was nondescript. It didn't look like it was from any particular decade. Very little color or personal items, but comfortable and clean. I had the feeling that Ben was the caretaker of this house rather than a resident.

His bedroom was on the main floor off the living room. I located the pants, shirts, and underwear he asked for, feeling a little like a voyeur even though he must be in his eighties. How our society conditions us.

I returned to the living room and found the book he was reading as well as a magazine of Sudoku puzzles by his beige, worn recliner. I started to turn away when a small photo on the end table caught my eye. It was a hand-colored portrait of a young woman with dark curly hair, blue eyes, and a flawless complexion. It was the girl I met on the beach in 1954—two days before.

Chapter Nineteen

I FELT DIZZY and disoriented and sat down hard on a footstool still gripping the picture. When I got my breath, I loosened the back on the frame. The back of the photo itself was yellowed around the edges, and written in faded ink was "Love, Minnie — July 1953."

I carefully put the photo back in the frame. Mom said Ben had never been married. Of course, that didn't mean that Minnie didn't exist. Apparently the romance had failed. What did the girl say? Her boyfriend had broken it off. Was Ben the boyfriend? But if he was the one who ended it, why would he concoct a story about a marriage, an accident and the death of his wife? That was the part that didn't jibe.

I returned the photo to the table and left the house with the bags. As I drove to the rehab center, I tried to determine an appropriate and non-hurtful approach to the subject with Ben. When I arrived, he was in physical therapy so I had more time to think.

I finally recognized that I didn't *need* to know the truth about any of it. I was curious and maybe the truth would help solve the mystery of the trailer but it wouldn't change anything. Ben was a respected member of the community who would do anything for anybody. I decided I would not either challenge or support the fabrication of his marriage. There was one question I could ask, though.

An orderly wheeled him into his room. "Lynne! Thank you so much for doing that."

The orderly helped him into his bed and left. As he arranged the blanket with his good hand, he said, "You know, after Minnie died, I convinced myself that I didn't really need family. I've had a lot of good friends through the years and we've helped each other when we needed it. But I'm finding it's much harder to ask friends to do things now that normally family members would take care of."

"Ben, I don't mind at all so don't give it another thought. How are you feeling today?"

"Better, I think."

"Good. Just don't be giving these doctors and nurses any trouble." I winked at him.

He waved his hand and scoffed at that. "I can follow orders if I have to."

The perfect opening. "Were you ever in the military?"

"Sure was—the army. Fought in Korea."

Bingo. Ben must have been the boyfriend who ended the romance with the girl on the beach. Why he pretended there had been a marriage I will probably never know. Maybe just regret, and he realized it too late. Perhaps Minnie had actually died or maybe just married someone else. We chatted about the town gossip and the upcoming Summer Festival. Finally I said that I needed to get home and fix supper and promised to stop back later in the week.

AT SUPPER, I told Dinah the story of the girl on the beach and the photo in Ben's living room. It appealed to every romantic fiber of her teenaged being.

"Wow. That is so sad. But why did he break it off if he loved her so much?"

I shrugged. "I can't ask him that. So we'll never know."

"His whole life." She shook her head. "It's affected him his whole life."

"Whatever happened, he must have acted hastily, and for some reason couldn't or wouldn't take it back."

"You wouldn't think one mistake would hang around like that." She shook her head again and I thought how much she still had to learn.

We talked about Ben a little longer and she headed to her room for homework, she said, although when I opened her door to tell her I would be out working in the trailer, she sat with headphones on, a movie or something on her laptop, and her fingers flying over the keyboard on her phone. Remember when 'text' meant the fifty-pound books you lugged home?

Anyway, she partially removed the headphones long enough to listen to me and say with a grin, "Don't fall asleep out there."

I made good progress on the paint over the next couple of hours and in another week had most of the paint removed. I scrubbed the walls all down one more time with steel wool dipped in stripper and washed them with a solution to remove any vestiges.

Meanwhile, we continued to visit Ben. The school year had ended and Ben taught Dinah to play cribbage. It was good for Dinah to have something to do in the summer. She was too old for a babysitter and too young to work. She occasionally babysat for our neighbor Jeanne Patterson, but she seemed to enjoy her time with Ben along with her regular trips to the library.

But in early June, it seemed to me he declined. He became impatient with his limitations and even snapped at me once—very un-Ben like. I reported on my progress with the trailer, but he almost seemed to take offense, so I found other topics of conversation.

Once the walls of the camper were clean, I rubbed a little stain over the wood to even the color and began finishing the walls with a water-based varnish. Dinah helped on Saturday and we completed two coats on everything.

Then we added our finds. Dinah was especially pleased with the breadbox and I got the brilliant idea to make new curtains out of old aprons that I'd found at Violet's. The profusion of patterns added a whimsical touch and a nice counterpoint to all of that wood. I had thought originally I would use a Thirties deco pattern for the curtain fabric but this was more fun. We were about ready for our next trip.

CHAPTER TWENTY

 YES, I HAD decided we would try it one more time. With reservations of a mental nature, but still. We stashed our 'new' clothes in the cute little drawers. I put the assortment of license plates in one of the storage areas and the set of pans in the cupboard.

We spent a couple of evenings with the atlas and the Internet looking for a park far enough away that we wouldn't be likely to run into people we knew but close enough that I could get us there and back. We finally settled on a place called Beggar's Bend State Park. The online photos looked beautiful, and again it was an old campground that had been built in the Thirties as a CCC project. A minor river wrapped around the campground and a small pond offered fishing and paddle boats. Well, they do now but who knows fifty-plus years ago?

I made a reservation and we planned several simple menus. On Friday, we both hurried home and were able to get on the road in a half hour. Dinah was wound up tighter than the key on a canned ham. Two hours later we followed a winding road down into a leafy paradise, with glimpses of dappled sunlight through the trees. The woods opened up at the bottom to a lovely stone and timber lodge with a spacious campground behind it surrounded by woods. A stream protected the area like a moat except that it was crossed by a quaint stone bridge.

Dinah, with the campground map gripped in one hand, directed me first to a water hydrant and then to our campsite. After we set up, she proudly heated canned soup and made grilled cheese sandwiches on the little stove. She said my mother was teaching her to cook. Well, good, she should teach one of us.

We decided to walk down by the river before dark. The blacktop road continued out of the campground, through some pines, to a slow lazy river. A picnic shelter with pillars and a fireplace built of the same stone as the lodge sat on the bank, so we perched on one of the tables to watch the river.

"Look!" Dinah said, pointing to the edge. A dark hump moved through the water and then got close enough that I could see the beaver's head just above the water with a stick clenched in his teeth. He seemed oblivious to us and went about his business, disappearing into the bank. Dinah had pulled her phone out of a pocket, but not fast enough.

"Oh, I hope he comes back out."

We watched for a while but with no luck. She wasn't discouraged though and put her phone back without even sending a text.

"This is a neat park."

"It is. I'd never heard of it before."

"Let's go up and start a campfire."

When we got back to our campsite, our neighbors, a middle-aged couple with a large new fifth wheel, were out and came over to ask about the trailer.

"Where did you ever find it?" the woman, who had introduced herself as Rhonda, asked.

I told her about Ben. "Would you like to see the inside? We've been working on it."

They followed me in as I gave them the history of our remodeling efforts, leaving out the parts about the time travel. They were fascinated by the icebox, although the husband, Brian, said, "I bet you could get a new one that would fit in that spot."

"I don't think I want a new one. We only go out for a couple of days at a time and this works fine — like a giant built-in cooler. I'm thinking of making the trailer an office for my travel agency anyway."

"How clever," Rhonda said with a big smile.

Back outside, Dinah had gotten a small fire going. Brian and Rhonda declined to sit with us and returned to their RV. Soon we noticed lights go on and the TV flickering through the windows.

"I don't even miss TV," Dinah said, with a little self-satisfied smile. Small steps.

We speculated about the other campers and made up stories about their circumstances. Dinah thought one man was camping with his twenty-something daughter but I said maybe she was a trophy wife. Dinah, who had been in a junior high performance of Oliver the year before, said that the Scoutmaster in the group camp area was probably training his troop to be pickpockets. And so on.

Neither of us wanted to be the first to suggest going to bed. Finally I said, "I went through this dilemma on the last trip. It's not too late to change our minds. We could hook up and haul the trailer back home. Sleep in our own beds."

Dinah shook her head. "I wanna do it. I wanna stay."

"Okay, one more s'more and that's it." I reached for the bag of marshmallows and offered her one.

CHAPTER TWENTY-ONE

 I WOKE THE next morning to the sound of hammers and shouts. I peeked through the curtains but couldn't see where the sound was coming from. Dinah slept on through the racket. The sky was gray and low, and the wind had picked up. I could see that Brian and Rhonda's fifth wheel was definitely not there.

I slipped into my 'new' slacks and blouse and went outside. Again, the campground was not in the same era as when we had gone to sleep. Gone was the asphalt covering on the road, leaving only dirt. Trees and shrubs were smaller, larger, or in different places. A number of canvas tents were in the campground, and across from us was another Covered Wagon.

But I was more interested in figuring out the source of the noise. I rounded the front end of the trailer and looked toward the stone lodge. Instead of a completed, beautiful building, there was only a foundation with stacks of stone and timbers scattered around the site. Men in drab gray loose pants and shirts worked on the building in small groups. What surprised me were the supervisors. At least two men stood by each group, wearing uniforms and armed. Obviously, the workers were prisoners. If we had ended up during the war years, could they be prisoners of war? I knew that especially German and Italian prisoners were brought to the Midwest. Or they could be from the nearby state men's prison. In spite of the guards, it made me nervous for Dinah's safety.

I returned to the trailer and fiddled with the knobs on the radio. Dinah stirred and turned over, shading her eyes with her forearm.

"Where are we?"

"Don't you mean *when* are we?"

She thought a moment. "Yeah. I guess." She got up and looked out the window.

As I turned the dial on the little radio, the initial static became interspersed with words. Finally I found a station that came in clearly. A clarion voice announced "The Breakfast Club with Don McNeill!" Harmonizing voices sang an upbeat song with what sounded like a full orchestra backing them up. While Dinah got dressed, I listened to the patter and finally gleaned an important tidbit. One of the cast made a reference to President Truman and the upcoming election. Ah. 1948. I told Dinah.

"So the War is over?"

Her history is a little fuzzy. "Yup — three years ago."

Over a light breakfast, I told her about the gangs working on the lodge.

She swallowed a bite of toast and said, "They're convicts?"

"Yeah, a lot of states have used prisoners on public works. I doubt if they let any serial killers take part, though. In any case, we'll stay away from that area."

I rummaged in the cupboard where I'd stashed the license plates and came up with a set of 1946 plates. Perfect. I found a black marker and made the 6 into an 8. I had attached small wire hooks for the plates so that I could just hook them over my current ones.

I handed one to Dinah to hang on the back of the trailer while I went to the front of the Jeep, and seeing no one watching, hooked it in place. We met back by the picnic table.

"Let's walk back down by the river and see if we see that beaver again. And there was a hiking path that went upriver we could take," Dinah said.

I almost expressed my shock at her suggestion but decided not to press my luck. "Sure. But it would have to be that beaver's ancestor. Best to get a walk in now in case it rains."

We followed the now dirt road down to the river. The pines along the road appeared to be new plantings.

"The shelter's gone!" Dinah said.

"Not gone—just not here yet. They've cleared the area and will probably build it when they finish the lodge."

There was a narrow, rough path leading north along the riverbank. Trees overhung the path and wild rose along the side threatened to reclaim it. A few places, I had to hold branches out of the way to prevent nasty scratches on Dinah's bare legs.

"It's getting cooler," Dinah said behind me.

"And the wind is picking up. We should probably turn around before we get caught in the rain."

"I'm going to stop at the stump up there. I think I've got a rock in my shoe. Wish I had my sneakers."

We continued to a small clearing. Dinah perched on a stump and pulled off her saddle shoe, shaking it out. As she was putting it back on, thunder rumbled, a drum roll heralding the big drops that began to fall.

She jumped up. "Let's go!" She motioned me ahead, just as a torrent hit. I was so intent on avoiding getting slapped in the face with branches or slipping in the mud, that I didn't notice additional noises off to the left. Sounds of crashing in the brush had just registered when Dinah screamed behind me. I whirled around to find my daughter, eyes wide, rain streaming down her face, and a sharp blade at her throat. A man in the drab prison garb held her with one arm around her waist and looked almost as scared as she did.

"I don't want to hurt her, lady, but I will if I have to." I could hardly hear him over the crashing thunder.

"Mom, don't let him…" Dinah cried.

"Shut up," he said.

A movement down the path. Another man in gray dashed across the open space and down the bank toward the river. Were we in the path of a mass escape?

"Please," I said. "We can't stop you. Let her go."

The rain pelted my face and I felt like I was in a car with bad tires on black ice. I had no idea what to do and was frozen with fear. He pulled Dinah with him backward down the path. I couldn't tell if there was more rain or tears running down my face. I felt stupid and helpless. I'm her mother, for God's sake, but I didn't know what to do. Tried to think and watched the almost frozen tableau.

I followed until he yelled, "No farther! Stop right there."

I stopped.

He continued backing down the path, taking Dinah with him. I stood there until he and Dinah disappeared around a bend. I edged slowly forward because I could still glimpse Dinah's white shirt through the trees at the bend. When I could no longer see her, I moved faster. At the bend, I peeked around the trees. Nothing. The path was empty. They may have disappeared around another bend or maybe he cut through the trees.

"Let me by, lady," said a low, calm voice behind me. I jumped and turned my head enough to realize that this man was one of the guards. I backed to the side of the path, at same time saying to him "Listen, he's got a knife, and he's holding it at my daughter's throat."

He wiped the rain off his face with his hand and took a deep breath. "Okay. That changes things." He sidled past me and continued down the path, gun drawn but down at his side. I followed and we had only gone a short distance when we could see them down in the river. The prisoner was dragging Dinah along the edge, the knife still at her throat.

"Swanson!" the guard yelled. "This isn't going to work."

"Sure, it will."

"She'll just slow you down. Let her go."

"It doesn't matter how slow I go if I have her." Swanson grinned, but his hand was shaking. The hand with the knife. I could hear dogs baying in the distance over the sound of the storm. Dinah looked, if possible, more terrified at the thought of being dragged along on his escape. But he continued to slosh along the river.

The guard moved down the bank. Swanson yelled, "Stay there! Don't come any closer!"

The guard stopped.

I didn't think Swanson saw me. A loud crack in the trees high above drew all our eyes up. Nothing appeared to be crashing down on me so I slid into the trees toward the bank, about twenty feet from Swanson and Dinah and ducked behind a giant cottonwood.

I had a better view of the river and spotted another escapee wading upstream. I peeked around the tree. The guard continued to talk to Swanson but remained where he was. Did he or Swanson know there was another man coming up the river? Swanson's eyes didn't leave the guard. I needed to stop the other man from coming to his aid. I tried to edge down the bank without slipping in mud, tripping on a root, or attracting attention in any way. The sandals I was wearing didn't help.

The other prisoner spotted Swanson, Dinah and the guard. He increased his pace staying close to the bank. I was too late. There was no way I could reach him before he got to them.

I could still hear the dogs but they seemed to be headed away from us. Surely other guards would follow the men who headed to the river, but I didn't hear anyone.

The other prisoner came up behind Swanson and the guard yelled, "Stay away!"

Swanson laughed. Not a very confident laugh, but a laugh nonetheless. "You're not going to make me look."

I had started toward the river again when the other prisoner grabbed Swanson's knife arm and managed to twist it back. Swanson let loose of Dinah to fend off his attacker. She dived for the bank and I stumbled into the water to reach her.

I pulled her away from the men just as two other guards clambered down from the path onto the bank. They disarmed Swanson and dragged him back up to the path, where they handcuffed him. Dinah threw herself at me, sobbing.

The first guard ordered the prisoner who had saved Dinah to put his hands up and pushed him up to the path. He was handcuffing the man when Dinah and I reached the path.

"Wait!" I said. And to the man who had stopped Swanson, "Thank you."

He shrugged his shoulders. "I have a daughter," he said simply, and cast his eyes down.

Chapter Twenty-Two

 THE FIRST GUARD, whose nametag said 'Jorgensen,' gave instructions to the other two to take the prisoners back to the construction site and then turned to us.

"Are you staying at the trailer camp?"

I nodded.

"I'll escort you back. We may still have other rabbits on the loose."

He turned to Dinah. "Are you all right, miss?"

Dinah nodded but gripped my arm and remained silent. I said, "We had just started back to the campground when that guy came out of the trees. Dinah was behind me and he just grabbed her so quick..." I couldn't finish.

"I'll get you back with the others and talk to you about it after we nab the rest of 'em. Maybe the rest of the guards already have but I want to be sure."

He gestured for us to go ahead. Dinah clung to my arm and I tried to see into the woods through the rain as we stumbled along.

When we reached the cleared area intended for the shelter and started up the road, I asked, "What happened? How did they get loose?"

110

"The storm. Lightning hit a tree near the construction and a branch fell on our transport truck. In the confusion, about seven men took a powder."

I told him about the prisoner I'd seen cross the path right after Swanson grabbed Dinah.

"Probably trying headed for the river to cover his scent from the dogs. He'll stay in the river for a ways but we'll be ready for him."

I hoped that his confidence was well deserved.

We reached the campground and when I pointed out our camper, he shook his head. "Please go over to that picnic shelter where the rest of the people are. There's an armed guard there."

The shelter was at the end of the campground, and although the rain had subsided some, Dinah was still shivering.

"Can I just get a blanket for my daughter?"

He nodded and waited with Dinah while I ran to the camper. When we got to the shelter I thanked him. He shared a few words with the other guard, pointing at us, and then hurried off.

Most people sat on the tops of the picnic tables, feet on the seats like they would be safer if they didn't touch the ground. They stared at us as I wrapped Dinah in the blanket, no doubt because of her red eyes and tear-stained face.

The guard came over. He was a short stocky man with reddish hair and almost a baby face. His nametag said 'Sturms.'

"Sounds like you are lucky stiffs."

"Yes. Do you think they'll catch them all?"

"They already have, all but one. The guy you saw head for the river?"

"Yeah. I didn't watch where he went because I was so afraid for Dinah."

He nodded. "I understand. Don't you want to sit down?" He motioned toward the picnic tables.

We sat on the end of the nearest bench, my arms around Dinah. She was still shaking and buried her face in my shoulder. A thin, worn looking man leaned against a post smoking. He wore green work pants and shirt, the right sleeve empty and pinned up to his shoulder.

"She all right?"

"She will be," I said, rubbing her shoulder.

He pitched the cigarette out in the grass and dropped to his haunches, still resting against the post. "Damnedest thing. I was in North Africa..." he nodded at his missing arm, "Lost this at the Kasserine Pass—and I was more scared this morning. I'm not sure most of those guys are even that dangerous. Obviously one was. But my family's here too. I can't imagine what you went through."

"Thank you," I said.

"Dad!" A boy of seven or eight with blond short hair and wearing jeans and an orange striped shirt ran up to him. "One of those prisoners captured a *girl* and *cut* her *throat!*"

Dinah looked at me with a little smile. The man put his hand on the boy's shoulder. "No, son, that's not quite true. She's sitting right over there by her mom."

The kid turned around with his mouth open. "Wow," he said. "Is that true?" He walked over and stared at Dinah.

"Yeah. It wasn't much fun."

"Wow," he said again. "Did he cut you?"

"Perry!" His dad said. "Leave her alone."

"It's okay," Dinah said, straightening up a little. "No, he didn't cut me."

"What did you do?"

"Whatever he told me," Dinah said. She was handling this well. Other people in the shelter had started to move closer or at least pay attention. Questions came from all sides and Dinah looked around in shock as the crowd seemed to be closing in on her.

Sturms, the baby-faced guard, moved closer, faced the crowd and put his hands out. "Okay, folks, let's give her some room." People backed off a little and Dinah withdrew back into her blanket.

"Sorry, ma'am," he said to me.

"We understand," I said.

"Sun's coming out," Dinah said.

Sure enough, the area on the east side of the shelter began to brighten with spotty sunlight.

People began to venture to the edge of the shelter and look out hopefully toward their tents and campers. A few moved toward Dinah and gave her a thumbs up or made general comments like "Good job" or "Glad you're okay."

Finally after another half hour, the guard Jorgensen was back. "They got him," he said. "He had made it to the highway and was trying to hitch a ride. You can let people go back to their campsites," he said to Sturms.

Then he turned to Dinah and me and said, "Can I have a few minutes?"

We sat down at a table facing him and he pulled out a small notebook. While he leafed through it looking for a blank page, I tried to think what I could tell him and what I couldn't. I was thankful that the computer age hadn't arrived, which meant it would be difficult for him to check what I told him.

"Can you give me your names?" he asked, looking directly at me.

"My name is Lynne Kelly and this is my daughter, Dinah." I spelled Lynne for him and he wrote it down, giving me a chance to check Dinah's expression. It hadn't changed; we had discussed before this trip that we needed to avoid giving anyone much accurate information about our names or hometown.

"And where do you live?"

"Des Moines."

"Are you okay, Miss Kelly?"

Dinah nodded. "Just scared."

He closed his notebook and patted her hand. "Well, you're a brave little girl."

Dinah winced slightly at the 'little girl' but the guard apparently thought it was just a reaction to her experience. He got up and stuck the notebook back in his pocket.

"I need to help get those guys back to their cells. We won't be working around here any more this weekend." He headed back to the construction site.

Dinah raised her eyebrows. "Not very thorough."

"In our time, they would have been very worried about liability and asked for our life stories. But that hasn't become a concern yet. Let's go get some dry clothes."

The shelter had emptied out and as Dinah stood up, she grimaced at the squishing sound from her saddle shoes. "These are going to take a while to dry out."

"True," I said, "but I think we've earned a little nap time."

"I doubt if I can sleep."

"I know, but you can read or we can play cards or something."

"I need a shower."

I grinned at her. "Time to learn how to take a sponge bath."

She stuck out her tongue and flipped her hair out of her eyes. My Dinah was back.

CHAPTER TWENTY-THREE

WHEN WE RETURNED to the camper, I took the wet blanket from her and draped it over the picnic table. She untied her shoes and tugged them off, setting them on the bench in the sun. I got a bucket of warm water and she hung her head down while I poured enough water for her to work up some suds and then helped her rinse it.

After she towel dried it and combed it out, we fixed some water in the sink and I left her to figure out a sponge bath. The day was turning quite nice, warm but not hot. I took a book out to read in the shade and became so engrossed that almost an hour passed before I heard the door open and Dinah came down the steps.

I expected her to be wearing one of the dresses we had purchased at Violet's because we only got one pair of shorts for her, but what I saw reminded me that my daughter could still surprise me. She had put her jeans on but rolled the bottoms up in wide cuffs about halfway up her calves. A short sleeved white blouse was tucked in and she had fixed her long hair in a page boy with wavy bangs. She carried a pair of bobby sox to put on when her shoes had dried.

"Well, look at you!"

She smiled slyly. "I was looking at a couple of the girls in the shelter. This is apparently an in-outfit and hairdo."

"Definitely," I said. "You were very observant. Great job."

"I kind of like my hair this way."

"Maybe you can start a 'new' style at school."

"Maybe I will."

"Are you feeling a little better?"

"A little. It helps being clean. Mom, how did that guy get a knife if he was a prisoner anyway?"

"I don't think it was a actually a knife. It was some kind of tool or implement that he had sharpened."

She grabbed my wrist and turned it so that she could read my watch. "Only 1:00?"

"It's been a busy day. How about some lunch?"

We went inside and proceeded to make some sandwiches. As we ate, I could see Dinah beginning to droop as the shock and adrenalin drained away. We decided a nap was in order for both of us and reconverted the dinette to a bed so that we both could rest comfortably. I dropped off wondering if the time change thing could happen during the day.

I slept the sleep of the dead for over two hours. When I opened my eyes and got oriented, I realized the dinette was returned to daytime use and Dinah was gone. My thoughts picked up from when I fell asleep with an added concern: what if one of us changed times and the other didn't? Something I had never considered that hit me now like a low doorway. I bolted to the door and realized simultaneously that I could hear voices outside.

Dinah sat at the picnic table with her back to me. Across from her was another young girl similarly attired but with her light brown hair braided in two pigtails. Dinah turned at the sound of the camper door.

"Hi, mom! Remember Perry over at the shelter? This is his sister, Peggy."

Relief rushed over me that nothing untoward had happened as I greeted Peggy.

"Gosh, Mrs. Kelly, that was just awful what happened to Dinah! I would have died of fright!" the girl said. I almost looked around to see who she was talking to until I remembered my new alias.

"I think I almost did," Dinah said. I could tell she was starting to enjoy her new notoriety.

"It wasn't something I want to go through again, any time soon," I said.

"And you had to stand and watch! My mom would have flipped a wig."

I was hoping that Dinah had been circumspect in her conversation with Peggy. I guessed the fact that Peggy hadn't flipped her own wig meant that Dinah hadn't said anything yet that raised questions.

"So where do you go to school, Dinah?" Peggy said, turning to her.

"Um, I go to a private girls school in Des Moines."

"Girls' school?" Peggy said. "That's a bum rap."

"I don't mind," Dinah said.

"But no boys?" Then Peggy noticed that I was still listening and blushed. "I mean, I guess that's okay."

I was pretty sure Dinah had never even talked to anyone who went to an all-girl school so I hoped she didn't get in too deep here.

Peggy rattled on. "That prisoner escape was the most exciting thing we've ever had happen when we were camping. I mean bad exciting, not good exciting. Usually we camp at the state parks but one time we stayed at a trailer park where they had a guy park your trailer for you and then move your car to a parking lot. Isn't that neat? Sometimes my mom and dad get pretty mad at each other trying to park the trailer. 'Course, it's harder since Dad only has one arm and he gets depressed easy so Mom tries to be patient. Do you wear uniforms?"

"What?" Dinah said, obviously as confused as I was.

"At your school. Do you have to wear uniforms?"

I nodded over Peggy's head.

"Oh. Yeah, we do," Dinah said. "It's not so bad."

"I 'spose. You don't have to decide every day what you're going to wear. Do you have a record player? We have big one at home but I'm saving my babysitting money to get a portable. I like Frankie Laine and of course, Sinatra. How about you?"

I could see confusion on Dinah's face after the words 'record player' so decided a rescue was in order.

"Dinah, we're going to cook hot dogs over the fire for supper. Maybe Peggy would like to join us?"

"Oh, I'd love to!" Peggy said. "I'll ask my mom."

"Of course," I said. "Dinah, will you get the fire started?"

"Sure." Almost a sigh of relief.

Peggy jumped up from the bench. "I'll be right back and then I'll help."

While she was gone, I explained that a portable phonograph was like an early iPod, only less portable, and gave Dinah a crash course on pop singers of the Forties. She committed a couple of names to memory and I suggested that if anything else came up, to keep in mind that Peggy was pretty easily distracted. When time traveling, one always needs a backup plan.

Peggy returned with her parents' permission to dine with us. She and Dinah took charge of cooking the hot dogs while I mixed up a fruit salad—using fruit cocktail of course—and got out plates, flatware, napkins, buns and condiments. I also decided to heat up a can of beans with a few additives and briefly regretted the absence of a microwave.

I could hear Peggy chattering away outside. It sounded like nothing was required of Dinah but a few grunts now and then.

I made a few points when we sat down to eat and Peggy said "Oh, fruit cocktail—my favorite!"

"Peggy, where does your family live?" I asked.

"Just over in Springville. We come here quite a lot. Sometimes my cousins come too but none of them are here this weekend. Uncle Bud farms and he's pretty busy this time of year. They aren't going to believe what they missed this weekend." Then she tried to tone down the excitement in her voice a bit. "I mean how awful it was and everything."

Dinah smiled at her. "That's okay. It's definitely an experience I will never forget."

Peggy turned serious. "No, I guess not. Do you want to go for a hike after supper?"

Dinah just looked at her for a moment. "Noooo, I don't think so. That's what we were doing this morning when I was nearly killed." She couldn't quite keep the sarcasm out of her voice.

"Oh! I'm sorry. I didn't mean anything—I mean, the prisoners are gone and they caught them all…" Peggy trailed off and looked down at her plate.

Dinah relented in the face of the poor girl's embarrassment. "I know. I'm just not ready to go out in the woods again yet. Do you want to play cards? Mom's been trying to teach me a couple of games."

Peggy nodded, still flustered.

"There's a chocolate cake in that cake carrier in the cupboard," I said.

"Yum!" Dinah said, trying to smooth things over. She got up with her plate. "Want some Peggy? My mom makes the best chocolate cake."

"Sure. Can I help?" They stacked up the dishes and carried them to the camper. By the time they reached the door, Peggy was going a mile a minute again. "Have you seen *The Treasure of Sierra Madre*? I just love Bogart, don't you? I wish I could go to the movies every night."

After our cake, I sat by the fire while the girls played cards at the picnic table. Many of the campers were out walking along the road, enjoying the beautiful evening and unwinding from the tensions of the day. Peggy's parents were among the walkers and ambled over when they reached our campsite.

"Nice evening," her dad said. "I'm Paul and this is my wife, Marilyn." He bobbed his head toward Peggy. "Has she talked your leg off yet?"

"Nice to meet you—again. Please join me. I'm sorry, I only have two chairs..."

Paul waved his good arm. "No problem." With one hand he stood a log on end and perched on it, motioning Marilyn to the other chair.

He put a cigarette in his mouth and lit it, inhaling while he returned the lighter to his pocket, and then grabbing it out of his mouth to exhale.

"How's your daughter?" he asked quietly. Peggy looked up from her cards, alarmed I think, that I might report her awkward comments.

"Better, I think. Still pretty shaken up."

"That was quite a scare," Marilyn said.

"Yes, it was," I said.

Paul sat up and forced a smile. "Well, I tell you, our Peg was pretty excited to find someone her own age here. Usually my brother and his wife camp with us but their kids are all younger. Just so she doesn't drive you crazy." He made a talking motion with his hand.

I laughed. "Oh, no. She and Dinah have enjoyed exchanging their experiences, I think."

Peggy gave me a little smile of thanks and said "Dad, Dinah goes to a private school. All girls!"

"Maybe that would be a good place for you," Paul said. "You could concentrate on your classes." He smiled again, more relaxed now. Peggy was obviously the apple of his eye.

"This is a beautiful park," I said to get away from the girls' school subject before we stepped in it.

"We love it," Marilyn said simply.

"More and more, we just need to get away from the world." Paul shook his head. "I thought after the war, all of that killing and dying would bring us some peace but it just gets crazier."

"What do you mean?"

"Oh, everywhere. These new countries this spring— North Korea and Israel. They won't last. The Arabs will stomp Israel out of existence in no time. And atomic bombs! What if Stalin gets the bomb? You'll think you haven't seen anything with Hitler."

"Oh, I hope not," I said.

"I hope not too, but I'm afraid that's wishful thinking," Paul said.

Marilyn put her hand on Paul's knee. "Honey, we're not 'getting away from the world' if you insist on talking about it. You just get all worked up."

Paul sighed. "You're right, I know." He stood up. "How about it, girls? Can you teach an old soldier that game?" The girls willingly made room for all of us and together gave us very broken and incoherent instructions. Of course, I had taught Dinah the game, which was a good thing because I would have been lost otherwise. We played for over an hour before Marilyn announced it was time for them to locate Perry and turn in for the night. It was a very enjoyable way to end a stressful day.

When we went inside, Dinah seemed preoccupied. Finally she said, "You know, people talk about the good old days, but they weren't always so good, were they? I mean, I thought after the war everybody would just be so happy to have it over but then they had new things to worry about."

"You're right. That's why a single TV show or movie that only focuses on one aspect isn't a very good source of history. Remember the old story about the blind men and the elephant? Each one only examined one part of the elephant and based his image on that."

She nodded. Time travel is certainly good for stimulating thought.

"I wanted so bad to tell them that the world wouldn't blow up and that Israel would survive."

"Would you also tell them that they have more wars to look forward to and about diseases like AIDs?"

"Probably not." She sighed. "After today, if we make it back this time, I think I will be content to stay there."

I agreed with her. It didn't seem the time to point out that scary things happen in our own decade.

CHAPTER TWENTY-FOUR

AFTER TWO SUCCESSFUL returns to our own time, I was somewhat confident that it would work again, but even a little doubt with so much at stake is enough to make sleep difficult. I tossed and turned on my couch and could hear that Dinah was restless as well. Sleep finally came and when I woke the next morning, bright sun was peeking through the curtains. I sat up and looked out the side windows. Brian and Rhonda's fifth wheel sat proudly in the site next to ours. I let out a huge breath, not even realizing until then I had been holding it.

Dinah was still asleep and I was sure she needed it. Although I had gotten in a good nap the day before, I didn't think she had. I set about making some coffee as quietly as I could and took a mug outside. There was no sign that they had had any rain the day before and the air was heavy. I sat for a while watching the campground wake up and decided a shower was in order. When I returned, Rhonda was wiping off the vinyl cloth on her picnic table.

"Hi!" she said, shaking out the rag. "Where'd you guys go yesterday? I wanted to invite you over for dessert last night."

Think fast. Was the trailer still here or wasn't it? "We had a family emergency." I hoped I sounded like it was serious enough that I didn't want to talk about it. And I wasn't lying—having your daughter held at knife point should qualify as a family emergency.

"But your Jeep was still here. It looked like your trailer was all locked up."

Aha. One question answered. "My brother picked us up in the middle of the night and brought us back late last night. His wife was very ill but seems to be doing better."

"Oh, well I'm glad to hear that. I was just worried about you." She laughed. "I'm glad you weren't transported away against your will!"

Well, not exactly against our will...

"Yeah, it made this trip kind of a waste. We were hardly here and now we need to head out early this morning," I said.

"That is a shame. But when family calls, we answer, right? It was nice meeting you. Maybe we'll run into each other again."

I thought, depends on which decade you camp in, but I said, "Great to meet you too. I hope we do see you again."

I went inside and dried my hair with the blow dryer we hadn't dared to bring out in 1948. Dinah was awake and as relieved as I was to be back 'home.' After she dressed and had breakfast, we packed up and headed out.

"I wonder how Ben is doing," I said, partly wondering out loud and partly for the sake of conversation.

"When did you see him last?" Dinah asked.

"Friday on my lunch hour. He seemed to be getting forgetful and crabby. You know Ben; that's not him. He's always been good natured, whenever you see him or whatever the circumstances."

"Did you ask him about the picture?"

I shook my head. "I decided that it would just be to satisfy my curiosity. I don't want to upset him for that."

"You're right. But I sure wish I knew the story."

"Me too."

AS WE UNLOADED the trailer at home, Dinah stared at the pile of vintage clothes.

"What are we going to do with all of those?"

"Wash the ones that need it and then I think we'll just leave them in here. I'm going to go ahead with making this my office and maybe I'll make throw pillows out of some of the fabric."

Dinah nodded without comment and made a laundry pile which she stuffed into one of the Toy Story pillowcases.

"It's been quite an experience," I said. I didn't think it would be good for either of us to lapse into the silence of denial like we had after the first trip.

"Yeah." She looked up at me. "I'm glad we did it. Really. I don't want to do it again, but I mean, a bunch of dates really doesn't teach us much about history, does it?"

"No. But you're okay? That guy grabbing you. That was horrible for both of us."

"I think I'm okay. Not sayin' I won't have nightmares about it. I need to try to remember that it could have been a lot worse." She shuddered.

I hugged her. "Right. And thank God it wasn't."

We finished hauling in food and laundry. Dinah said she had homework to do and I decided I'd better go see how Ben's weekend had been. Dinah said she would lock the doors after I left, which I understood.

BEN LAY ON his back with his head turned away from the door, looking out the window. He appeared to be awake but at first I got no response from him.

"Ben? How are you feeling?"

"Who?"

"It's Lynne."

"Min?"

"No Lynne. From church, you know."

"Oh."

I sat in the chair beside the bed and took his hand.

"How is the physical therapy going?"

"The what?"

"Exercises to help your arm."

He rubbed his arm. "Okay, I guess."

He tried a feeble smile. Then his face cleared and recognition dawned.

"Lynne! Have you been camping?"

"Yes. We just got back."

"How was it?" He raised his head to look at me more closely.

"It was-uh-nice. A state park called Beggar's Bend. We'd never been there before."

"We? Did you get Dinah to go?"

"Yes. Actually, it was her idea." I decided to take a chance. "Ben, when you—and Minnie—camped in that trailer, did you ever end up somewhere else?"

"What do you mean?" His lips tightened up and his eyes clouded over again. Much to my alarm, he gave a little sob. "I took her back."

"Took who back?" I was completely confused.

He started shaking his head continually, like at two-year-old might. "She's okay, she's okay," he said over and over.

An orderly appeared in the doorway. "Mr. Walker? Are you okay?"

I stood up. "I don't think he is. He suddenly became very confused and I don't understand what he's saying now." That was true. Was 'she' the trailer? I didn't know. But I did feel guilty that my question seemed to trigger it. No way I was going to try and explain the question to the orderly. Two nurse's aides rushed in behind him and I backed up so they could get to the bed.

They talked to Ben and fussed with tubes and devices so I said, "I'll wait outside."

I sat on a chair in the hall and put my head in my hands. I vowed I would never ask Ben another question about the trailer. It was obvious that he had had some kind of unusual experience with it and was upset that we had something happen too.

The staff came back out of Ben's room and assured me that he was resting comfortably. It was time to go home and see how Dinah was doing.

CHAPTER TWENTY-FIVE
Dinah

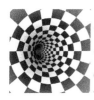 DINAH SLEPT RESTLESSLY, dreaming about being chased in a rainstorm, but whether it was the escaped prisoner or someone else chasing her, she couldn't be sure. When she woke, she started picking up her room. What better way was there to take your mind off time travel and abductions than cleaning?

She heard her mom come in from visiting Ben and call up the stairs. She answered and continued with her assignment.

At supper, her mom reported on Ben's problems and his reaction to her question.

"What do you think he meant?" Dinah asked.

"It may have just been a delusional reaction. But he sounded like it was something he felt guilty about, something he regrets. I don't know what he meant."

Dinah was tired of trying to figure it all out so she changed the subject. "I'm going to Dad's next weekend, right?"

"Yeah. Why? Is that a problem?"

"No. Just wondering. What are you going to be doing?"

"I've got a bus tour to Chicago Saturday and Sunday."

"Good." She hoped her mother would give up on this camping business or at least in that trailer. Her mom just looked at her oddly but didn't say any more.

ON TUESDAY, DINAH walked down to the library. Summer had arrived with a vengeance and the cool library provided welcome relief from the heat and humidity. She had just finished a time travel romance that she thought was pretty dumb. The main character spent more time panting after this guy than trying to get back to her own time. Having been through the trauma of being displaced in time, she couldn't get how a girl could spend so much time admiring a guy's muscles in the midst of all of that turmoil.

As she wandered through the stacks, she looked around for Bret but didn't see him. She decided to tackle Stephen King's *11/22/63*, although it was a lot thicker than anything else she had read. As she stood in line to check the book out, she scanned the study tables. No one she knew. When she realized Miss Simpson was watching her, she blushed and ducked her head down. It was like the old busybody could read her thoughts.

She pushed open the heavy entrance door and ran smack into Bret and a wall of warm air.

"Dinah!" he said with that warm smile. He glanced at the book in her arms and raised his eyebrows. "That should keep you busy awhile."

She shrugged and pulled back into the entrance, motioning him inside. "You said it was pretty good."

He nodded. "Lots of stuff about how minor actions by time travelers can have lasting effects." He smiled again. "Well, let me know how you like it. We can talk about it after you're done—someday over coffee?"

"Sure," she said. "See you later."

She walked on home.

CHAPTER TWENTY-SIX

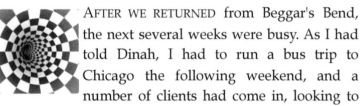 AFTER WE RETURNED from Beggar's Bend, the next several weeks were busy. As I had told Dinah, I had to run a bus trip to Chicago the following weekend, and a number of clients had come in, looking to schedule some kind of vacation before summer was too far gone. We both helped with the summer festival at church and Dinah did some babysitting for Jeanne Patterson. There were green beans and tomatoes in the garden to freeze.

In the trailer, I had pulled back a corner of the old brittle linoleum and found brown and cream checkerboard tiles underneath. So I proceeded to remove the rest with a putty knife and great care.

Meanwhile, Ben had not improved. Dinah stopped a couple of times to play cribbage only to be met with a silent face that didn't seem to know her. She hadn't known either Kurt's dad or mine so Ben had become kind of a substitute grandfather for her and she was taking his decline hard. On the other hand, she seemed to resent it when I would go to visit him. Go figure.

She spent quite a bit of time at the library and not as much time as usual with her friend Tish. Kurt reported that she seemed extra moody during the weekend she spent with him, although it was hard for me to conceive of what extra moody with Dinah would be like.

So I wasn't surprised when my mother called and asked about Dinah.

"Maybe she could come have lunch with me someday," she said.

"I'm sure she'd love that. She seems kind of lost this summer — and moodier than usual."

"Is it boyfriend trouble?" Mom asked.

"I don't know. Why do you ask?"

"Well. You know I don't like to gossip, Lynne." That was true; she didn't. "But Arlene Simpson told me the other day that she has been meeting an older boy at the library."

"How much older?" My insides clenched and I thought of several times that I had mentally questioned the time she was spending at the library.

"Like college age." More clenching.

"When you say 'meeting'…."

"Just talking, I guess. Except that she thinks at least once, they had coffee on the patio. Hardly a sin, and I do think Dinah has more common sense than we usually give her credit for. But Arlene was just concerned because there was such an age difference."

I sighed. "She does usually have a good head on her shoulders." I thought of our recent trip. "But she's also pretty vulnerable this summer with our separation."

"Well, just giving you a heads up. See if she wants to have lunch Thursday. We'll go out. I'll pick her up at 11:30 unless she lets me know differently."

"Okay. Thanks, Mom."

Dinah came home shortly from babysitting. I decided to try and open the lines of communication.

"How are things going, honey?" Nice, neutral start.

"Fine." Nice, neutral response.

"Grandma Linda called. She wants to take you out for lunch Thursday."

"Great."

"If you have something else, you need to call her."

"I said great." Neutral, but not so nice.

"Dinah, I know you've been spending a lot of time at the library.'"

"So now that's a sin?"

"Of course not. You've been doing a lot of reading on time travel. Is that helpful?"

"What do you think? It's fiction."

What happened to neutral?

"Don't get so defensive. I'm just interested."

"You haven't been until now. Wait—Grandma called —she's friends with Miss Simpson—library—" She snapped her fingers and pointed one at me. "She narced on me, didn't she?"

"About what?" I tried to act innocent—not something I've had a lot of practice at.

Big sigh, flipping the hair back, rolling the eyes. "The *guy* that I've talked to there. I knew Simpson had to stick her nose in. He's interested in time travel books and has given me some recommendations. That's *all*. He's way older than me."

"I know — that's why the concern."

"Well, there's no need for concern, okay?"

I hesitated. "Maybe it would be best if you avoided him. He may not see the relationship the same way — "

She actually stomped her foot. "What? There is no relationship! I know what I'm doing and you don't need to tell me how or what to do. It's not like you're so great at relationships anyway!" She was yelling and her face was red. I held up my hands in sort of a surrender but she would have none of it, burst into tears, and took the steps two at a time up to her room. The slam of her door punctuated her exit.

I collapsed in the recliner, emotionally exhausted. That little scene hadn't gone exactly as I had planned. I wondered if Dinah had told this guy about our own adventures. I was pretty sure she wouldn't for fear of seeming crazy, but I wasn't positive. This didn't seem to be the time to ask her.

I dozed a little, and then went to the kitchen to finish making supper. When it was ready, I went up and knocked on Dinah's door. No response.

"Dinah? Supper's ready, honey."

Silence.

"It's meat loaf and baked potatoes — your favorite."

"Not hungry," was the muffled reply.

I went back downstairs and ate alone. About 9:00, I was reading out on the screen porch, trying to gain solace from a beautiful sunset when I heard her come downstairs and go into the kitchen. The refrigerator opened and closed, a couple of cupboard doors banged, and I waited for her to come to the porch, cooled off enough to talk. Instead, she went back upstairs and slammed her bedroom door again. Not as loudly as before but still making a statement. Maybe my mother would be able to get through to her when they went out to lunch. I went to bed.

Chapter Twenty-Seven

 Early the next morning I sat on the porch with my coffee and made a list of things I needed to get done during the day. It was a perfect summer morning, one that I would much rather spend in my flower garden than in my office but the realities of life said otherwise.

I hoped Dinah would be up before I left and we could talk things out a bit. I wanted to tell her that I remembered a few incidents blown all out of proportion in my youth and that, if that was the case here, I was sorry. Parents' fears are often magnified in the light of their own experiences. Finally, I got dressed for work, and before I went downstairs, decided I would see if she was awake. I knocked softly and opened the door.

While the spread was mussed, her bed appeared not to have been slept in. She was not there. I tried to control my fear as I hunted around the room. Her backpack and phone were gone. So was her iPod. I looked in her closet but couldn't tell if anything was missing.

I sat on the bed and tried to collect my thoughts. Maybe she went to her dad's. I rushed downstairs for my phone and called Kurt.

"Are you still home?" I blurted out as soon as he picked up.

"Yeah. What's the matter?"

"Dinah's gone. Is she at your place?"

"No. I would have called you if she was. Are you sure she's not there?"

"Yes!" I almost shouted. "Sorry. We had an argument last night and she wouldn't talk to me the rest of the night. Spent the evening in her room."

"What was the argument about?"

I told him what Mom had heard from Arlene Simpson. Kurt also knew that my mom doesn't gossip, and a possible threat to his little girl got his interest.

"I'll be right over."

I had an appointment with a regular client that morning so I called him and postponed. Then, waiting for Kurt, I searched the house more thoroughly for any signs of where Dinah might have gone. For some reason, as I looked around the kitchen, I opened the refrigerator. The leftover meatloaf was gone. I remembered her in the kitchen the night before and going back up to her room. Had she taken it all then?

A scrap of paper on the bottom shelf caught my eye. A green sticky note, spotted with grease, had the words "Don't look for me" written on it. I almost laughed at the melodrama of it all. Like I was going to just say "Oh, okay," and go on with my life.

But then it hit me that this was pretty extreme even for Dinah. Kurt burst in without knocking — not surprising, I guess, since he had lived here for fifteen years or so. Kurt is a clothes horse and prides himself on his grooming, but today he had only gotten as far as khakis and a white t-shirt. His light brown forelock hung down to his eyes instead of carefully brushed back. He was worried too.

"Have you found her?"

I resented his almost accusing tone. "No, I haven't found her." I held out the note. "This was in the refrigerator."

He took a breath. "Makes me wonder if there isn't something to the gossip. Have you called Tish's house?"

"No. Why don't you do that and I'll call Mom. I hate to worry her but that might be where she'd go."

"But," Kurt brandished the note, "she knows your mom would let us know right away. If she really doesn't want to be found, at least for a while, she wouldn't go there. Do you know anything else about this guy at the library?"

I shook my head. "They open at 9:00. They have photos now of all of their patrons. But if I ask Arlene Simpson for information about him, she'll contact Mom for sure. We need to think about this."

I poured him a mug of coffee and let him add the sweetener. "Let's sit down at the table." I picked up a notepad and pen by the phone. I could tell that he realized too that rushing into a search might have repercussions that we didn't want. We took chairs across from each other and I was sure that the sadness in his face was mirrored by my own. The French doors open to the porch framed a scene fit for a greeting card with the wicker furniture and dappled sun playing on the garden beyond but it couldn't lift my spirits.

Kurt pushed his hair back and folded his hands on the table. "Maybe this is just wishful thinking, but it seems most likely she would go to a friend's. She wants to scare us and it's working. Start your list with Tish and let's put down anyone else who is a possibility."

"We can eliminate several. Courtney's at camp and Morgan and Brianna live too far out in the country."

"Is her bike here?

I walked out to the back porch and looked at the side of the garage. "Yes."

When I came back in, Kurt was punching buttons on his phone. After a couple of minutes, he laid his phone on the table. "No answer on her phone."

We listed five or six other good friends we thought might be candidates for Dinah's hiding out. They all had parents who worked during the day so no questions would be asked, at least for a while.

"We have to talk to your mom, if only to cross her off," Kurt said.

"Okay." I took a deep breath. "If none of these pan out, I think we have to face that she may have hitchhiked out of town or else is with this guy from the library. So we need to report it to the police. I don't think we should try and find that guy on our own."

Kurt rubbed his forehead with the heels of his hands. "I hate to get the police involved, probably because I hate to think we *need* to do that. But I think you're right."

We divided up the list of friends to call. Two of them did not have landlines and weren't in the phone book, but one was the daughter of a woman I'd met through the soccer team and I had her number in my phone. We quickly made our calls with no luck and then got in Kurt's truck to drive to Beth's house, which we had no phone number for. He waited while I went up to the door.

I looked around after ringing the doorbell and didn't see any suspicious activity at the windows. A young boy whom I assumed was Beth's younger brother finally opened the door.

"Hi!" I said with more cheerfulness than I felt. "I'm Dinah McBriar's mother. Is Dinah here?"

He shook his head and then turned and bellowed "Bethie!"

Beth came around the corner and pulled off her headphones. "Yeah?"

"She's looking for Dinah."

"Dinah left this morning and I forgot to ask her where she was going. We have a family emergency and need to find her." I gave a helpless little 'silly me' laugh.

Beth shook her head. "I haven't seen her. Did you try her phone?"

"She must have it turned off."

Beth gave me a look that said no teenager would ever willingly turn her phone off. "Sorry."

I thanked her and returned to the truck.

Kurt leaned his head against his door when I reported the visit. "Call your mom, I guess."

I dialed Mom and gave her the same story I had used on Beth, leaving out the family emergency. I hung up.

"She hasn't seen her either," I said.

He started the truck. "We have to go to the police, don't you agree? They can issue one of those Amber Alerts."

I nodded and my eyes started tearing up. Kurt leaned over and patted my hand. "We'll find her."

The small police station that served our little town was exactly what one would expect on a lazy summer morning. A receptionist was showing another young woman a magazine article and one man in uniform sat at a desk to one side, looking bored.

"Help you?" the receptionist said, holding her place with a finger.

"We need to file a missing persons report," Kurt said.

The receptionist looked back at the man at the desk, who stood up and said, "Come back here, please."

We followed him through the main room to a small office. He sat behind the desk and indicated the visitors' chairs.

He pulled a form out of the drawer and said, "Now, who's missing?"

The reality of it hit me hard.

Chapter Twenty-Eight

 I LOOKED HELPLESSLY at Kurt, unable to speak.

"Our daughter, Dinah McBriar."

He gave the officer a short, precise account of Dinah's disappearance.

"Has this ever happened before?"

I shook my head. "No. Never."

"I need to get your vital information, here. Name and address?" He looked at Kurt. Kurt complied.

The officer looked at me, pen poised over the form. I gave him my name and address. He looked from one to the other of us.

"Divorced?" His voice was edged with suspicion.

"Separated," Kurt said.

He leaned back in his chair. "So are you sure this isn't a custody issue? One of you have her stashed somewhere?"

"No!" I said. "We are both scared to death."

He picked up his pen again. "Has she ever been threatened or anything?"

I thought not in this decade but also that neither he nor Kurt would understand that at this point. Maybe not at any point.

I said, "No. But we are concerned about a young man she has been — visiting with — at the library. He's apparently college-aged and she's only fourteen."

He raised his eyebrows. "Arlene Simpson tell you about this?"

"She told my mother."

He made a note. "Well, I'll check with her but she can tend to exaggerate."

"We know. And I hope that's the case here."

He asked for a photo. Kurt got one out of his billfold and gazed at it a moment before handing it over. We also gave him a description.

He stood the forms up and tapped the edges on the desk and then clipped the photo to them.

"I'll get Shelly to get this alert out right away." He stood up and offered his hand. "I also need to see her room. Is there any chance that someone could have come in the house in the night and abducted her? I mean, I think we're looking at a runaway, but we have to consider every possibility."

I explained how our bedrooms are only separated by the small stairway landing. "I'm a pretty light sleeper. I don't see how anyone could have gotten her out without me hearing them. The steps are bare wood and they squeak — you can't go up and down them quietly."

"Are you going to be there in about fifteen minutes?"

"I can be," I said.

"Okay, I'll be over to take a look around."

We left the station with some relief and some sense of unfulfillment. I realized I was hoping the officer would be able to pull her out of a hat — or even a jail cell.

We drove back to my house and waited for the police search. Officer Muller, true to his word, was there in less than fifteen minutes. I showed him Dinah's bedroom. He checked the windows for any sign of entry and found none. We also pointed out the door locks and I assured him that I locked both doors every night.

He scratched his head as he clipped his small flashlight back on his belt. "Well, I don't see anything that indicates she was taken from here. Let me know of anything you hear that might be useful and I'll keep you updated."

We agreed and he left.

"Now what?" I said to Kurt.

"I think the best thing for both of us would be to go to work. Keep busy. We gave them our cell numbers. I'll stop by the house about 5:00."

I started to protest. Something seemed basically wrong about going on with our lives as usual but my practical side had to admit he was right. We had driven around town earlier in an attempt to spot her with no luck. It's a small town; there just aren't that many places to go.

I changed my clothes and packed some snacks in a lunch bag. At my office, I rescheduled the appointment I had missed that morning for right after lunch. I went through the mail and updated some files on the computer.

Since I was a one-woman operation, I had some filing to get done and I also tried unsuccessfully to put together a mailer about a fall leaf trip. My client appeared on time and we spent the better part of an hour planning a winter trip to Brazil for him and his wife. By the time he left, I was a frazzled mess.

I decided to close up for the day and walked the block to the police station.

The receptionist looked up and evidently recognized me, as she gave me a sad smile.

"Hi—" I read her desk plate, "—Sondra. I was in this morning..."

"Yes, I know. The missing girl."

"I thought I would stop before I went home to see if there is anything new."

"I don't think so, but I'll get Officer Muller." She knocked on the door of the office Kurt and I had been in, and the officer came out to the counter.

"Have you heard anything?"

"Ms. McBriar, we'll contact you. I know this is hard. We've put an alert out. I'm questioning Bret Burns right now but he doesn't seem to know anything. He doesn't even have a car."

"Who's Bret Burns?"

"The young man she met at the library."

I gripped the counter. "He's back there? Can I see him?" I had convinced myself that someone else must be involved.

"No. That won't help matters any at this point. He rents a room in town and we have searched that and found no sign of your daughter."

"Thank you." I didn't know what else to say. I couldn't think. I walked back to my office and drove my Jeep home.

Once home, I poured a glass of iced tea and took it out to the porch. I thought back to the argument that started this. Like many such events, it seemed so innocuous. It certainly seemed to me that Dinah had overreacted. I wasn't trying to be a dictator, just giving gentle advice.

The fact that she had reacted the way she had made me question the innocence of the relationship. Officer Muller was very circumspect about giving me any information about Bret Burns or letting me see him. I went in the house and grabbed the phone book. Of course he wasn't listed. He probably just had a cell phone and maybe had only moved here recently. Maybe I should talk to Arlene Simpson.

Kurt pulled in the driveway. It was only about 2:30.

"I couldn't concentrate," he said when he reached the porch. "I don't suppose you've heard anything either?"

"No, nothing," but then my cellphone rang and I grabbed it.

"Hello?"

"Lynne, it's Mom. I just got an Amber Alert on my phone for Dinah. What's going on?" She sounded frantic.

I mentally smacked myself in the head. "Oh, I'm sorry, Mom. I should have called you and never thought about it being sent out that way. It's been an awful day." I described the confrontation with Dinah the night before about the young man at the library and the ensuing argument.

"This morning she was gone. The police have questioned that guy and don't think he was involved."

"That's why you called this morning looking for her."

"Yes, I hoped she turn up soon and didn't want to worry you."

"I'm coming over."

I started to protest but knew it would do no good.

"Okay." I hung up.

"Your mom?" Kurt said.

"Yes. She gets Amber Alerts on her phone. I should have called her." I was suddenly overwhelmed with feelings of being the worst mother and the worst daughter in history and burst into tears.

CHAPTER TWENTY-NINE

"YOU CAN'T DO everything," Kurt said.

"No, but I'm not handling this well at all. If Mom hadn't gotten that notice, one of her friends probably would have told her and that would have been worse."

"But she did get it. Don't worry about something that didn't happen. You have enough on your plate."

"We have enough," I corrected.

"Yes, but you have your mother to worry about too."

I needed a hug from somebody so I threw my arms around his waist and buried my face in his chest. He pushed me gently back by the shoulders, alarm in his face and asked, "Has something else happened?"

"Nothing. That's the problem." I told him about my visit with Officer Muller.

"So it sounds like Officer Muller doesn't think this Bret guy is involved."

I shook my head. "They searched his room and found nothing."

"He could have taken Dinah somewhere out of town during the night."

"He doesn't have a car."

"More difficult but not impossible."

"No."

Mother opened the side door and called in "Lynne?"

"Come in." I poured her some tea.

Kurt!" she said, giving him a hug. "Good to see you." I always suspected that she liked Kurt even better than me and she hadn't been any happier about the separation than Dinah had.

"How've you been, Linda?"

"Fine, fine, except for this. I'm worried sick about Dinah, as I know you both are."

"Let's go out on the porch, Mom."

We brought her up to date with our progress — or lack of progress — so far. We discussed possible actions. Kurt thought he might drive to the nearby truck stop on the Interstate and show her picture around. We agreed that either Mom or I would be at the house at all times in case of calls on the landline. I thought I should visit Ben and my mother said that when I got back, maybe she would go to the library and see what she could find out from Arlene Simpson.

Kurt grabbed his truck keys and almost ran into Officer Muller who was about to knock on the door.

"Do you have news?" Kurt said.

"Nothing definite. They're holding a young girl answering your daughter's description over in Silverton. She doesn't have any ID and she says her name isn't Dinah, but that doesn't mean much. It's hard to know —

there's a lot of averaged sized teenaged girls with long blond hair."

Kurt brightened. "But it could be her?"

"Possibly," Muller said. "Can you drive over to see if it's her?"

"Absolutely."

Silverton is the county seat about twenty-five miles away. Kurt thanked the officer and turned to us.

On the drive over, Kurt was keyed up.

"She needs to understand how much worry and grief she's caused us."

"Easier said than done," I said. "Teen-aged girls are notoriously self-centered."

"Do you think it's because of our split?"

"Part of it, I suppose. But some of it just goes with the territory, I'm afraid."

He glanced over at me. "Would you be willing to consider counseling?"

"For us or Dinah?"

"Us."

I looked at him in surprise. I had suggested that back when we first separated and he brushed it off at the time.

"Certainly. I told you that before."

He smiled and nodded. "You were right."

My spirits inched upward. Maybe this could all work out for the best.

The police station in Silverton was in the back of City Hall. We explained our presence to the receptionist and a female officer standing behind her ushered us back to an office remarkably similar to Officer Muller's.

A young girl slumped in a chair, hair and build like Dinah's, but not Dinah. I sagged against Kurt and shook my head at the officer.

"That's not her," I said.

The policewoman who had followed us said. "I'm sorry. Thank you for coming. I hope you find her."

The ride back home was much quieter. Kurt seemed lost in his own thoughts and I stared out the window.

When we got back to the house, Mother was waiting. Once again, I had been so wrapped up in myself, I hadn't thought to call her. Her face drooped when she saw we were alone.

"It wasn't her," was all I could get out. She knew what to do. Sometimes you really need a hug from your mom. She needed one too. And Kurt joined in. We all wiped our eyes — dust or something.

"Well, now what? Should I still go to the truck stop?" Kurt said.

"Why don't I go?" Mom said. "Then you and Lynne can be here and ready to go if the police call again."

"Linda, I hate to have you go around tapping on truck drivers' shoulders and..."

"You think they'd rather talk to you or a little old lady that reminds them of their mothers?" She grinned at him.

He relaxed and smiled back. He took a photo of Dinah out of his pocket and handed it to her. "You got me. Go get 'em."

"I'll just get my purse." As she went out the door, she said over her shoulder, "I have my phone. Call me if you hear anything!"

WE RETURNED TO the porch, phones arranged on the table. Kurt put his head in his hands and then looked at me. "But where else would she possibly go? I mean, if she went on her own? I know she's been rebellious and thinks we're stupid about most things, but I don't think she has the confidence to strike out completely on her own, do you?"

I had to admit that I couldn't see that either. "I guess you never know."

Kurt stared out at the back yard. "Maybe she's hiding in your old trailer," he said, a hopeless little smile on his face.

I almost choked on my swallow of iced tea. "Kurt! You don't think…" He could see the alarm on my face.

He was still smiling. "Wouldn't that be just the ticket? If she's been hiding out there the whole time?"

"You don't understand! Oh, no—I never thought after the last trip —that would be awful…"

"What are you talking about?" He had stood up, about to go out to the trailer.

I caught myself. "Let's check the trailer first."

CHAPTER THIRTY

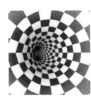I RUSHED OUT the screen door toward the trailer, tripping over my own feet a couple of times. Kurt followed.

I opened the trailer door and called in through the screen. "Dinah?" No answer. We went in.

She wasn't there and obviously there are no hiding places. I looked under the benches just to be sure. However, the dinette was made into a bed and the Toy Story sheets were rumpled.

Noticing this, Kurt said, "She probably just slept here and is out roaming."

"I'm sure she is. The question is whether she's roaming in this decade or some other."

"What?"

"Let's go back to the house and sit down. You aren't going to believe what I have to tell you but I swear to God it's true. If Dinah was here, she could back me up, but then, if she was here I wouldn't have to tell you."

We walked back to the house. "What are you talking about?" Kurt was struggling to control his temper.

"The trailer. That I bought from Ben Walker." And I went on to tell him about the trip to Parson's Grove and what happened the first night Dinah and I slept in it. I explained about the shower house that disappeared and the outhouses that stood in its place the next morning. I told him about the couple in the vintage trailer and the registration forms filled out with '1962.' I described the man I had never seen before, coming out of this very house when we drove into town.

He shook his head. "Lynne, it was a dream. The power of suggestion. Maybe the vintage trailer you saw and then when you slept, you dreamt about it."

"That's not true. That trailer wasn't there until Saturday morning. There was a modern motorhome there the night before. Dinah and I remember the same details. The boy who was hunting for Russians because Kennedy was 'too weak.' The huge old elm trees in the campground. The cars on the road. The farm fields instead of new houses on the edge of town."

"So if that is all true, how did you come back? Why aren't you still there?" His smirk was so irritating, except that I knew I would react the same if the situation was reversed.

I told him about the box of jewelry and how Dinah had been wearing a bracelet that I thought was from the early Sixties. "So she didn't leave it on Saturday night and we were back in the present the next morning."

"Lynne, don't you see how crazy this is? It was one time and that's easily explained as a dream or hallucination or something."

I sat forward. "Kurt, why do you think Dinah has been reading all that time travel stuff this summer?"

That stopped him. Dinah had taken her library books with her when she stayed with him.

Then he said, "Maybe that's what gave you the idea. Although I can't imagine what you're trying to accomplish. This is a waste of time when we should be concentrating on finding her."

"I am! Don't you see? I need to sleep in that trailer tonight. I think that's where she went last night. Maybe she was just hiding and didn't think it would happen if the trailer was just here in the yard. Or maybe she really wanted to time travel. Anyway, it wasn't just one time." In for a penny, in for a pound. "I took it out myself when she went to stay with you. I ended up in 1954. I was accused of being a Commie sympathizer. And then Dinah wanted to try it again. She had read enough that she wasn't frightened any more and wanted to really experience another time." I explained how we had bought vintage clothes and license plates and took the trailer to Beggar's Bend. I decided not to get into the prisoner escape and the abduction at this point.

"You're nuts, Lynne. You've always been the down-to-earth, practical one. But you've lost it."

"Look, I know it's a lot to swallow. After the first time, Dinah and I didn't even talk about it. We both believed that it hadn't actually happened and that we were losing it. That's why I tried it a second time. But, I am going to sleep out there tonight and see what happens."

I told him my theory about removing the layers of remodeling and how it affected the time the trailer returned to. "I just removed the linoleum that was put in during the Forties. Now it's the original floor. If she made a trip last night, it should be to around 1937, when that trailer was new."

Kurt threw up his hands. "I give up. I believe that you are convinced, but that doesn't make it true. I suggest we order a pizza and wait to hear something from the police."

I agreed to go along with that much of his plan. He called the local pizza place while I checked for messages everywhere: Facebook, cell phone, land line, and email. Nothing.

We had our pizza on the screened porch at the old round oak table. I had scrounged a couple of beers out of the back of the refrigerator.

By this time, I figured I couldn't shock Kurt much more, and partly to take our minds off our missing daughter, I told him about Ben's phantom marriage and the photo of the girl I had met on the beach in 1954.

He chewed his pizza stoically and I thought he had decided that my flights of fancy weren't even worth commenting on any more. But finally he said, "I've never heard of Ben being married. He told you he was?"

"Yes, and that they were in a terrible accident in the Sixties, she had serious injuries and was confined to a wheelchair. She died soon after from the injuries."

"Well, he wasn't originally from here but he's been around since I can remember. Maybe that all happened when he lived somewhere else. Did you ever tell him what you think happened when you slept in the trailer?"

"Not exactly. I asked him once if when he and Minnie camped in it, they ever ended up somewhere else."

"And what did he say?"

"He got real confused and said something about 'I took her back.' I don't know for sure what he meant."

CHAPTER THIRTY-ONE

WE WERE BOTH silent for a few minutes. I pushed away from the table.

"I'm going to get stuff ready for tonight. I need to make sure I have some basics in the trailer." I paused and looked at Kurt. "I would like to have you stay out there too but I don't imagine you want to do that."

He looked outside at the trailer. The fading light gave it almost a foreboding look. "No, I don't want to. I don't want to encourage this whole crazy thing. But I don't want you to be alone either. I'll think about it."

I took our plates and the pizza box in to the kitchen, saving the rest of it for Mom. I heard Kurt come in and go into the living room. When I finished cleaning up, I went in to see what he was doing. He sat on the couch, leafing through one of the scrapbooks that I had put together about Dinah. Tears were leaking down his face. He gazed at a page that recorded a visit we had made four years before to a wax museum.

In the photos, Dinah hammed it up beside figures of Elvis Presley and Joseph Stalin. We had asked another tourist to snap a shot of the three of us standing by Michael Jackson. We all looked so happy.

Kurt looked up at me. "What happened to us?" He replaced the book on the coffee table and stood up. "I'm going to get some overnight things. I'll sleep in the trailer too." He put his hand on my shoulder. "When we wake up in the morning, and we are still in the here and now, we will focus on working with the police to find her, okay?"

I nodded. I was very sure that Dinah had slipped back through the time portal. But if he was right, and that was not the case, it was a reasonable plan. Maybe she would return to us overnight. That was an alarming thought.

"Kurt! What if she comes back to the present while we go back to the past?"

He controlled his face. "We'll ask your mom to stay here." His tone was the one he had used to reassure Dinah when she was four. At least now I knew how he would treat me if I suffered from dementia later in life. If there is a 'later' for the two of us.

"I'll be right back. You'll be okay?"

"Of course."

BUT BEFORE HE left, Mom got back from the truck stop. She shook her head hopelessly. "No one has seen her."

I warmed up her pizza and we went back to the porch. "Mom," I said, "I need to tell you something."

She stopped chewing and looked up at me in alarm.

Kurt sat off to the side as a signal that he wasn't going to comment either way. I took a deep breath and launched into my narrative.

"You are not going to believe this, but I swear it's all true and that it might explain where Dinah is." I repeated the whole story I had given to Kurt, again leaving out the prisoner escape. I also thought now that I should have burned that trailer after we returned from that trip.

Mother sat stunned. She hadn't touched her glass of tea. "Lynne, I would think you were pulling my leg but one thing you have never done is lie to me. But nothing in my makeup lets me accept this."

"I know," I said, waiting for more.

"Let's just assume for a minute that this all happened as you say. Where—and when—would Dinah have ended up if she slept in there last night?"

I told her my theory about the remodeling. "Every time we've been in the same spot that we started from. So she would be in this back yard, but almost 80 years ago. Was this house here then?"

"Yes, it was. It was built around the turn of the century," she said slowly. "No screen porch of course and the garage was built in the Fifties—around the time I was born. I think there was a small barn back there at one time. But Lynne, what would have happened if the camping spot you were in was occupied on the day you went back in time?"

"I hadn't thought of that. The first time was early spring and there was hardly anyone there. The second and third times I guess we were just lucky." This was getting worse.

"So what are you going to do?" Mom was good at cutting to the chase.

"I'm going to sleep there tonight, and Kurt says he's going to stay there with me." I looked at Kurt to see if he had changed his mind. He just nodded. "I wanted you to know in case you couldn't find us tomorrow."

She went pale. "No!" So a little piece of her believed me.

"There's a chance that if Dinah did travel in time, and she sleeps in the trailer tonight, she will be back here tomorrow morning. I'd like you to stay here in case she is."

"So why don't you wait?" She was bordering on hysterical. Kurt still didn't say anything but raised his eyebrows at me. He agreed.

I sais, "If she doesn't come back, it's another twenty-four hours before we can get to her."

My mother wasn't giving in. "And what is likely to happen, Lynne? She won't be in danger. From what you say, she knows how to get back. On the other hand, if this is just a fantasy or she did run away or was abducted in the here and now...what if the police need you tomorrow?"

I hate it when she makes sense. "On the other hand, what if she takes off from there? We'll never be able to find her. And she'll be so alone..." I whimpered, remembering the feeling of being in 1954 without anyone near and dear to me.

"Not if she shows up at this house. Your grandmother, Lynette Olsen, would have been 14 in 1937."

Her tone of voice raised a little alarm. "That's good isn't it?" I said.

"I hope so. There were some pretty crazy stories about my mom when she was young."

CHAPTER THIRTY-TWO

I STARED AT Mother. "What?"

"My Grandma Olsen told me about several times that Mother got in pretty big trouble." She stopped and stared into space a moment. "But, Lynne, if Dinah ran away and hitchhiked out of town, we are likely to hear something tomorrow. She isn't the type to cut ties with us forever and I'm sure by now is regretting her hasty actions. I think we will hear something from her tomorrow."

I wanted to believe her. It would be much simpler. But what she had just told us about her mother made me even more determined.

The house phone rang. Kurt rushed inside and grabbed it. Mom and I followed him but his side of the conversation was mostly "uh-huhs" and "I sees."

He hung up and turned to us. "That was Muller. There's nothing new."

I said, "I am definitely sleeping in the camper tonight."

To my surprise, Kurt didn't argue. "I am too."

"Well," Mom said, trying to keep things light, "I guess I'm stuck here by myself. You really should get a dog, Lynne."

"Right. I need something else I can't keep track of."

"This isn't your fault," Mom said.

"Then whose is it?"

"Dinah's," she said quietly. "She overreacted and left to punish you. Whatever happened, she instigated it."

I shook my head. "She's a child. I should have gotten rid of that trailer after the first trip. I just can't understand why Ben didn't warn me about it."

Kurt got up to clear the table. "There's no benefit in the blame game, Lynne. Let's focus on a plan. What do I need in the camper?"

I tried to do as he suggested. "Um, maybe just a pair of khakis and a white shirt? If you have a nice wide tie, that would be good."

He grimaced. "Okay. I'll go to my place, check email, and get some things. I just thought about money. It won't be much but I'll bring some coins from the Thirties and Forties out of my collection."

While he was gone, I decided I would run by and see Ben. Mother said she would stay near the phone.

I was pleased to find Ben sitting up and more alert than the last time I had been here. I kissed him on the forehead and asked him how he was doing. He waggled his hand back and forth. So-so.

"Ben, I have a couple of questions to ask you about Minnie, but I don't want to upset you. Is that okay?"

He actually brightened a little more. "No, shoot!"

"Were you married before you moved here?"

"Yup. Snapback County, north of here."

"And you came here after she passed away?"

He nodded. "Too many reminders there. The accident was my fault and I had to pass that spot too many times in my daily travels."

I patted his hand. "I'm sorry. What was she like?"

He smiled again. "Oh, I wish you had known her. She could cheer the saddest person up. She loved to dance and would try anything. Wasn't much of a cook though. But that was okay. I always loved to cook. There were a lot of fellas after Minnie Gunder, I can tell you that." He sank back against the pillows, a little smile of remembrance lighting his face.

"She sounds wonderful," I said.

"How's Dinah?" he asked. "She hasn't stopped by in a while." It wasn't accusing, just concern.

"Um, she's been busy," I said.

"Is she excited for school to start again?"

"Oh, you know kids, Ben. It's hard to tell."

We chatted a little longer and I left. I remembered then that Ben had told me earlier that he and Minnie used to sit out on the front porch of the house he lives in now. Something didn't jibe here. I had an idea about Minnie, but it would have to wait until Dinah was found.

WHEN I RETURNED home, I gathered up my toothbrush, pajamas and other necessities and threw them in a plastic grocery bag. I took them out to the trailer, and I fretted about my mother. I worried about what it would do to her if morning came and we were all gone. I set up the couch bed. Since I wasn't sure what would happen, I filled a couple of jugs with drinking water and put bread and lunch meat in the icebox. I made sure a couple of the house dresses I had found were ready to go. Finally I snapped on an antique gold locket that I hoped would do the trick.

Back in the house, I got sheets, a blanket, and pillow out and put them at the end of the couch for Mom. I gave her some towels and a toothbrush. I keep a supply of cheap ones on hand for Dinah's overnight guests who sometimes forgot to include theirs with their makeup. I almost choked at the thought. Everything led back to Dinah, even a throwaway toothbrush.

I joined Kurt and Mom in the living room to watch the late news. The Amber Alert was at the top of the broadcast. Seeing Dinah's school picture on the screen like that felt like a fist in my chest. When the announcer switched to a report on a house fire, I turned to Mom.

"Did Arlene Simpson know what Dinah talked about with this young man?"

She shrugged. "She didn't say."

"Dinah told me in our argument last night that he was just making recommendations on time travel books —that is his special interest. Feasible, I suppose. But she reacted so extremely when I suggested there might be something more that it made me suspicious."

"Rightly so, I think. But you said the police had questioned him and didn't think he was involved."

"Well, he doesn't have a car and he just has a single room."

"That would make it difficult, not impossible." Exactly what Kurt had said.

"I know. I haven't ruled him out."

"But you persist with this time travel thing. Why?" she said.

"It's as logical as any other explanation."

She smiled. "Did you hear what you just said?"

We said our goodbyes to my mother, who was trying to hide the fear she felt for our safety as well as Dinah's. We trooped out to the trailer. Both of us had books along, but I only read for about five minutes before I turned off the little pinup light.

"Good night, Kurt," I said.

CHAPTER THIRTY-THREE
Dinah

 IT WAS SO DARK in the camper when Dinah woke up, she thought it must still be the middle of the night. She groped around for her phone but couldn't find it. She then pulled back the curtains by the dinette bed and could see one vertical slash of bright light off to the side. That confused her. Swinging her feet down to the floor, she kicked her backpack and found the small flashlight that she had remembered to throw in. She switched it on and got up and walked to the door.

When she opened it and aimed the light outside, it reflected off an old wooden wall. A fence? No, a quick sweep with the light over her head revealed a high wooden ceiling with open beams. The camper was inside a structure—a barn or big garage of some kind. The slash of light she had seen from the window was a space between a couple of boards.

She had slept in her clothes, so she found her shoes, picked her way down the steps and used the light to find a door. One end of the building had large double doors but there was a small door tucked in the corner. She had to negotiate some old tools and barrels to get there.

171

She opened the door a crack and peered out. The bright sunlight blinded her momentarily but when her eyes adjusted, she recognized her back yard. Sort of. An old apple tree in the corner held a rope swing and the vegetable garden was in a different spot. Her house sat where it always had but instead of the screened porch, a few rickety wooden steps led up to the back door.

She pulled the barn door shut. She had done it. Time traveled on her own. She'd show her mom that she wasn't a kid any more. The idea that she was too dumb to know that an older guy wouldn't really be interested in her still made her furious. She went back to the trailer and found her pink shorts, white shirt, and her saddle shoes. She discovered some of the lights worked off the battery but when she plugged her curling iron in, the outlets did not work.

So she brushed her hair well and just pulled it back with a headband. That would have to do.

She closed the trailer up and went back to the side door. As she put her hand on it to push it open, a voice said:

"What are you doing in our barn?"

Dinah jumped, dropped her flashlight and turned around but couldn't see anything. There was rustling behind a stack of boxes. If not for the voice, she would have thought it was a rat.

"Who is it?" Her voice almost squeaked. Maybe she was the rat.

"Mind your own beeswax." A shadow rose up from behind the boxes.

"Excuse me?" Dinah said.

"I won't excuse you. You're trespassing." It sounded like a young girl — certainly not an adult.

"I'm sorry. It was an accident," Dinah said.

"Accident?" The voice came closer.

Dinah stepped back, right on her flashlight, but jerked her foot up quick enough to avoid breaking it and reached down and grabbed it. She flicked it on and aimed it at the girl.

The face almost made her drop the light again. It was familiar — very familiar, because the girl bore an eerie resemblance to herself. The blond hair, the short nose, the shape of the face, the hint of dimples.

"Who are you?" Dinah asked again. "Who *are* you?" She felt a chill. Was this some other kind of time warp where she had run into herself?

The girl shaded her eyes from the light. "You're pretty bossy for a trespasser." She pointed at the trailer. "Where did *that* come from? Why don't we go outside where I can see you, too? And you can tell me all about it." She paused. "Otherwise, I'll scream and my big brother will be out here in a flash."

Dinah backed away. "You go first."

The girl edged her way around Dinah to the door and pushed it open. She stepped outside and spun around to watch Dinah emerge. She gasped a little but didn't say anything at first. She just realized we look an awful lot alike, Dinah thought.

"First," the girl said, "how did you get that thing in our barn? My dad's going to blow his wig if he sees it."

173

"Does he go in there much?" Dinah asked.

"Only to get tools for something. But how'd you get it in there? You had to pull it with something."

Dinah sighed. "You wouldn't believe me."

The girl grinned. "Try me. Let's go out behind the barn where no one can see us."

When they got behind the barn, the girl turned to Dinah and crossed her arms. "Well?"

"I'm not from here," Dinah began.

"I know that. I know about everybody in town, 'specially my own age."

"No, I don't mean I'm not from this place. I mean I'm not from this time."

"Go on! That's nuts. So what time are you from?" The sarcasm oozed from her voice.

"2014," Dinah said.

"Sure. And I'm Shirley Temple."

"Who?"

The girl rolled her eyes. "Sonia Henie? Myrna Loy?"

Dinah shook her head. "I don't know who that is."

The girl studied her. "I don't believe you. Or you grew up in a tree."

Dinah said, "Please tell me your name."

"Okay. Lynette. Lynette Olsen."

"And you live in that house?" Dinah pointed.

"Yes. So?"

"So do I," Dinah said. She sat down on a stump and looked up at Lynette. "I think you are my great-grandmother. That's why we look so much alike."

"What? You *are* nuts!" Lynette looked almost frightened for the first time.

"I know what it sounds like. That trailer," Dinah pointed toward the barn, "was built in 1937. My mom bought it from an old guy in our church. And every time we sleep in it, we end up in an earlier time. Usually we take it to a campground and that's where we wake up, only years earlier. Last night it was parked out behind our garage. This barn isn't there in 2014. I slept in the trailer and woke up here. I didn't put the trailer in your barn; it put itself there."

Lynette shook her head. "No."

"Look," Dinah said. "There's two bedrooms upstairs in your house, right? Which one's yours?"

"The small one. Above the drive."

"Is there a cubby hole in the back of the closet? Lower right hand corner?"

Lynette stared at her with her mouth open. "You've been in my house?"

"I told you; I live in that house too—only sixty or seventy years later. Come back inside and let me show you something."

Lynette wasn't looking quite so sure of herself but followed Dinah into the barn and then into the trailer. Dinah fished in her backpack for her phone and held it up.

"Do you know what this is?"

Lynette shook her head.

"It's a telephone."

"No! Show me how it works."

175

"Well, it doesn't work here. In the future, they build tall towers and the signal bounces off of them and I think satellites in space and..." She could tell from Lynette's expression that she had lost her.

"Space? You mean like Buck Rogers?"

Dinah shrugged. "I never heard of him either, but by my lifetime, we have satellites and Americans have walked on the moon."

"When?"

"Um, I think about 1965. I don't remember for sure. Before my mom was born, I know that. Anyway, since there's no towers and no satellites yet, this phone won't work now."

Lynnette looked around the trailer. "This is pretty cool. Where are you really from?"

Dinah looked at her and held up the phone. "I told you. The future. Here, look at this." She pulled her iPod out of the bag and offered the earbuds to Lynette. "This is how we listen to music. Put these in your ears."

"In my ears?"

"Sure." Dinah turned it on.

Lynette listened just a few minutes before jerking the buds out of her ears, her eyes wide. "What is that?"

"Rock music."

"That's not music. Can it play swing? It's a radio, right?"

"What?"

"You know, Basie, Ellington, Benny Goodman?"

"It can play anything I download from the Internet. It's not a radio. It only has music that I put on it." Dinah punched a few buttons and pulled up "We are Young" by fun. "Try this."

Lynette watched the screen and put the earbuds back in. She listened and started moving to the music. This time when she took the earbuds out, she said, "That's cool."

"Now do you believe me?"

Lynette chewed the inside of her cheek. "Maybe I'm dreaming."

"Or maybe I am," Dinah said, "but this is the third time this has happened to me."

"You've been here before?"

"No, the first time it was in Parson's Grove. Ever heard of that?"

Lynette nodded. "It's a little park."

"We ended up in the 1960s when we camped there. Then we camped at Beggar's Bend and woke up in 1948."

"Why isn't it always the same time?"

Dinah explained her mother's theory about the remodeling.

Lynette put her hands on her hips and grinned. "Well, I don't care how you got here. I think we should have some fun. First we need to do something about your hair. It's too long. You look like a little kid. Got a scissors?"

"What?" Dinah said.

"A scissors? We need to cut it. I'll be right back." And she was gone.

Dinah sat there stunned and then picked up a hand mirror and studied her hair. It would grow back out. She didn't want to stick out.

Lynette was back with a scissors.

"Sit down—you got a hair brush?"

Dinah reached in the little bathroom for her brush. Lynette ran her thumb across the bristles.

"What is this stuff?"

"Um, plastic or nylon or something."

"Cool." Lynette removed the headband Dinah had put in a short time before.

"Have you ever cut hair before?" Dinah asked.

"Sure. I do mine all the time."

She did seem to know what she was doing and when she was finished, Dinah's hair fell just to her shoulders.

Lynette brushed the hair all back and then parted it on the right side. She then pulled a barrette from a pocket and used it to fasten all of the hair back from Dinah's face and forehead on the left side. She stood back and appraised her efforts.

"Much better. You're quite a dish, now. This gonna be fun. A little more curl at the bottom would be good."

"I have a curling iron but the outlets aren't working," Dinah said.

"You have a curling iron that plugs in?" Lynette said. She seemed more astounded by that than anything else Dinah had told her.

"Of course. How else would you heat it up?"

"On the stove, silly. We'll try yours later in the house. But for now, let's go down to Swan's—the drugstore."

"What for?"

"A Coke, of course. It's where everyone hangs out. I need to go get a dime from my mom."

"A Coke is a dime?"

"Two cokes," Lynette said.

"Well, I have a dime," Dinah said. She dug in her backpack and handed a coin to Lynette. She had about thirty dollars in baby-sitting money with her but it didn't seem prudent to reveal it all at once.

Lynette looked at the coin in her palm and held it out to Dinah.

"This isn't a real dime. This is the President. He's not on any coins."

Dinah peered at it. The profile on the coin looked familiar but she wasn't sure which president it was.

"Roosevelt," Lynette said. "It's FDR. There aren't any coins with him on them."

"He's president now?" Dinah asked.

Lynette rolled her eyes. "Uh-huh. You'd better keep your mouth shut to stay out of trouble." She laughed and led the way out of the trailer.

Dinah waited out on the sidewalk while Lynette went in the house. She could hear Lynette through the open window begging for the dime and promising to weed the garden for it. She would have to be very careful about everything she said.

CHAPTER THIRTY-FOUR
Dinah

ON THE WAY downtown, Lynette pulled a battered lipstick tube out of her pocket and turned a stub of bright red up. After she applied it while still walking, she said, "My mom is a pill about makeup. She won't let me wear any so I stole this from her old ones. Want some?" She held it out to Dinah.

"No, I have some."

"You should put some on. Sometimes there's some cool Joes at Swan's." She grinned. "Older guys who can't get jobs."

Great, thought Dinah, that's how I ended up here. Actually she was excited by this adventure. She'd stay just long enough to teach her mom a lesson and then go back. Meanwhile she'd enjoy herself. The houses along the way were familiar since Dinah (and Lynette) lived in the oldest part of town. Now most were white with white or black trim, often dingy and in need of paint, instead of the tans, greens and blues that the owners had painted them in the twenty-first century. The trees and yards varied, too but the same small town summer morning feeling existed. Lynette told Dinah she had two older brothers. One was working in a CCC camp and one was a janitor at a local factory. Her father worked nights at the same factory and slept during the day.

"I wish I could show my friends your music thing," Lynette said as they approached the main street. "But I know I can't. Nobody would believe this."

"I can hardly believe it myself," Dinah said.

Swan's was a single front store, one that Dinah had never paid much attention to. She thought it was an insurance office in 2014. It was cooler inside because of numerous ceiling fans. Shelves stretched along the front section and were stocked with every kind of medical and cosmetic necessity. Some brands were familiar to Dinah, most not.

About halfway back, a long soda fountain began, punctuated with green upholstered stools bolted to the floor. Most were occupied — a few business types having their morning coffee and the rest kids — young boys twisting back and forth on the stools, girls Lynette's age who greeted her as they passed. A couple of the young boys wore strange close-fitting hats with turned up jagged brims, festooned with buttons. Behind the counter, a young man in a snowy white shirt and paper hat filled glasses from a spigot and an older woman, also dressed in white, leaned on the counter and chatted with one of the business men. In the back, a row of wooden booths held more kids. Most of the girls wore cotton dresses with a few in shorts. A red haired girl in the back booth waved them over.

"Lynette! Who's your friend?" She moved over and patted the seat beside her.

Lynette plopped down and motioned Dinah to the other side next to a short girl with brown hair and glasses.

"What's the story, morning glory?" the short girl said.

"This is my cousin, Dinah. She's going to be staying with me for a couple of days. Dinah, this is Edith," she pointed her thumb at the red-head like she was hitchhiking, "and Bernie."

"You know," said Bernie. "You really look alike."

"People have told us that," said Lynette.

The waitress who had been behind the counter appeared at their booth.

"Would you girls like something?"

"Two Cokes," Lynette said, plopping down her dime.

The waitress scooped it up and said, "Be right back."

Edith nudged Lynette. "Look over there," she whispered.

All four girls turned toward the opposite side of the store where a counter held a display of razor blades and razors. A broad shouldered young man stood with his back to them, selecting a package of blades. All Dinah could see was his blue work shirt and black curly hair.

"Who is it?" Lynette said.

"That guy we saw at the fair last night—at the Ferris wheel," Bernie said.

"I bet he's been ridin' the rails and just hopped off because of the fair," Edith said.

"Probably looking for work," Lynette said.

"Or a handout." Bernie giggled.

"He can come to my door any time," Lynette said.

The young man turned and smiled at them, blue eyes crinkling. The return of the waitress with Lynette and Dinah's Cokes blocked their view.

"Girls!" The waitress admonished them at their groans of disappointment.

They ducked their heads and smirked at each other as they sipped their Cokes.

"Maybe we should go back to the fair this afternoon. Hang out by the Ferris wheel," Lynette said with exaggerated innocence.

Bernie frowned. "I have to do a 4-H demonstration at 3:30. But I'll bring some other clothes along. I'm not wearing that uniform all night."

"Hey, maybe we can come watch you," Edith said.

Bernie sat back and put her hands flat on the table. "Don't you dare! My leader would blow her wig. And I couldn't keep a straight face."

BACK AT LYNETTE'S, Lynette introduced Dinah to her mother as a new girl in town. Dinah hoped she could keep all of her stories straight. If her mother, Florence Olsen, noticed a resemblance between the girls, she didn't mention it. Instead, she smiled at Dinah and welcomed her, then handed Lynette a pot and sent her out to pick green beans.

Dinah remembered seeing photos of her own Grandma Linda with her grandmother, Florence--Lynnette's mother. They were grainy black-and-whites of an older woman, stern and in a dowdy looking dress with a young girl who didn't appear to be enjoying herself either. It was hard to identify that picture with this younger, animated woman who hummed while she bustled from one task to another. Very confusing. Florence wore a pink flowered cotton housedress with a full yellow apron of the type Dinah remembered wearing in preschool for art. She was canning green beans and frequently brushed her hair out of her eyes or used the corner of the apron to wipe her brow.

Dinah followed Lynette out and helped with the beans—a task she had done for her own mother many times. Flies and mosquitoes buzzed in the summer sun and once when Dinah was holding the pan, Lynette grinned and suddenly whacked the bottom of it, spilling the beans on the ground.

"What'd you do that for?" Dinah sputtered but couldn't keep a straight face as Lynette doubled up with laughter and pointed at Dinah's left ear. Dinah put her hand up and ran her fingers through her hair. A green bean fell out and she broke up too.

They finally got the pan full and carried it back in the house. Mrs. Olsen took the pan and dumped it in the sink. "Those will be good for supper."

"I don't think I'll be here, Ma. We're going to the fair with Bernie and Edith."

"Oh, honey, you were just there last night. And we can't afford for you to eat down there."

"We're packing sandwiches for our supper." News to Dinah.

"Oh." Mrs. Olsen sighed and then smiled at them. Dinah had a feeling that she was a pushover for anything Lynette wanted to do.

Dinah said goodbye, walked down to the corner of the block, continued around the corner to the alley, and followed it to the barn. She and Lynette had already planned that she would sneak back to her trailer, make herself lunch and change her clothes. Mrs. Olsen would think she had gone home.

It was funny; she wasn't averse to trying to pull one over on her own mother but she felt a little guilty doing it to Mrs. Olsen, who after all, was her own great-great grandmother.

The dark of the barn was a welcome respite from all of the uncertainty and tension of the morning—watching every word she said and every move she made. She fixed a sandwich out of the leftover meatloaf. She had put it in a little cooler with ice from home and put the whole thing in the camper icebox. But the ice was melted now so it seemed prudent to throw the rest out.

After lunch, she lay down on her little bed and, in the midst of rehashing the morning in her head, dozed off.

A knock at the door and the sound of it opening startled her awake.

"Dinah!" Lynette said in a loud whisper.

"Come in. I just took a little nap."

"Little? About two hours," Lynette said. "Are you ready to go?"

"Sit down. I will be in a sec."

"Sec?"

"Second, I mean. Sorry." Dinah pulled the blue checked dress from the cupboard, after she saw that Lynette had a dress on.

"Clothes haven't changed much in your time," Lynette said.

"Oh, this? We got it at a second-hand store. I hardly ever wear dresses in my time. Just jeans and shorts most of the time."

Lynette fingered the fabric and noticed the label at the neck. "Nice. Store bought. I've never had a store bought dress."

Dinah was surprised at that but didn't comment. She removed her shorts and blouse and reached for the dress.

"Wow!" Lynette said, eyes wide. "Underwear sure has changed. Does your mom know you have that?"

Dinah grinned as she slipped the dress on. "She bought it for me."

"Wow." Lynette said again. "Let's try that curling iron of yours, Ma's gone so we'll have the house to ourselves."

They trooped into the house and worked on each other's hair and critiqued their makeup, finally exchanging approvals. Lynette grabbed her purse.

"Let's go. Edith will be waiting for us."

"Wait. What about our sack lunches?" Dinah said.

Lynette scoffed. "I'm not taking a sack lunch to the fair."

Dinah hesitated. "I have some money but I don't know if we can use it. Someone might get suspicious."

Lynette patted her purse. "I borrowed some money out of Ma's jar. She sells some of the stuff she grows in the garden so, really, we worked for it." And she was out the door.

CHAPTER THIRTY-FIVE
Dinah

 WALKING TO THE fairgrounds, they had to cross the railroad tracks. Dinah noticed a man carrying a cloth bundle lurking furtively around the work area.

"What's that guy doing?"

"Hobo," Lynette said, matter-of-factly. "He's probably going to hop a freight. Not too many bulls around here."

"Bulls?"

"Railroad guards. They try to keep people from riding the rails, but I don't think they have much luck."

"Like that guy in the drugstore this morning?"

"Yeah—some of them are pretty young and dreamy. There are even some girls. There was a movie a few years ago, *Wild Boys of the Road*, where they tried to scare kids from doing it, but I think it would be fun."

"Lynette! Why would you leave home to do that? It sounds scary," Dinah said.

Lynette stopped and faced Dinah. "You did it. Why did you? You think it's scarier to hop a train than travel through time?"

Dinah nodded. "You're right, but it sounds scarier to me."

Lynette started walking again and said over her shoulder, "Some day I'm going to do it."

Edith was waiting inside the gate of the fairgrounds, licking a Slo Poke sucker and gazing at a sideshow in a wooden wagon labeled in garish letters across the top, THE GIRL WITHOUT A BODY. The side of the wagon was open and a piece of black cloth ran from the bottom front of the opening diagonally to the upper back. In the center of the cloth was a girl's head, smiling and chatting with the crowd, her face framed in short dark waves.

Lynette tapped Edith on the shoulder, who without looking away, said, "Look at that!"

"I saw it yesterday," Lynette said, pulling her friend on down the midway. "It's a trick."

Dinah thought, of course it's a trick. Do people believe this stuff? She looked at the crowd as she followed the girls. Many of them looked convinced. She also noticed with surprise the number of men in dress slacks, white shirts and hats. Others, probably farmers, sported clean overalls and plaid shirts, but still wore hats. Women wore dresses and often hats, some even gloves. On the other hand, in spite of the spiffy dress code, the grounds seemed to be covered with trash.

Other sideshows lined the midway as they walked along and barkers hearkened to passersby about the wonders of the dog man, the incredible pretzel twins, a bearded lady and other sights. As they passed the 4-H building, Lynette poked her head in the door, spotted

Bernie, and stuck her tongue out at her. When they reached the cattle pavilion, Lynette coaxed the others inside and then flirted shamelessly with several high school boys getting ready to show calves.

Bernie caught up with them when they returned to the midway. They were standing by one of the games that involved throwing darts at balloons. She was dressed in a long blue skirt and baggy middy blouse with a long black tie. She carried a paper sack.

"Wait for me here. I need to go change out of this monkey suit."

Lynette nodded and Bernie took off.

Lynette led the way past some of the other games. Dinah caught up with her. "She wanted us to wait for her."

"She'll find us." She stopped. "Do you see what I see?"

Edith and Dinah turned in the direction she was looking. The young man from the drugstore was running a ring toss game. Lynette sauntered over and pulled a nickel out of her pocket.

"Lynette!" Edith whispered. "Don't you dare!"

Lynette put the nickel on the counter. "Hey, handsome, think I can win that kewpie doll?" She struck a pose, one hand on her hip and thrusting her rather small chest forward.

Dinah stood back, speechless at Lynette's brazenness. The young man, however, was appreciative. He grinned and his face crinkled around his very blue eyes. He wore a cap set at an angle on his black curls, reminding Dinah of the lead actor in the performance of *Carousel* that she and her mother had gone to at the local community college

"Well, kitten, if your arms are as good as your gams, you shouldn't have any trouble." He winked at her, laid three colored rings on the counter, and picked up her nickel.

Lynette covered her mouth with her hand, as if she was shocked, which of course she wasn't. She tossed one of the rings and it fell short, falling on the ground.

"Oh, silly me."

She picked up another ring and the young man leaned over the counter and gently took her wrist. He moved it back and forth in a sideways motion a couple of times and then said, "Let it go."

The ring flew at the targets that were colored pegs protruding from a board, but bounced off one and fell back to the ground. Lynette clapped her hands.

"Almost!" she said, and looked up at the young man with shining eyes and a pretty blush.

Oh brother, thought Dinah, and hoped she wasn't that obvious when she flirted with boys herself.

Bernie appeared behind Edith and Dinah as Lynette picked up the third ring. She started to give it an underhand toss, but the young man guided her wrist into the side motion again.

"Remember, like this."

He let go and stood aside. Lynette appeared to concentrate so hard that the tip of her tongue peeked through her lips and she tossed the ring expertly, landing on one of the pegs. "She's the pitcher on our softball team," Edith whispered in Dinah's ear.

The young man handed Lynette a little celluloid doll.

She smiled at him and said, "You aren't from around here, are you?"

He shook his head, folded his arms and leaned against the post. "I'll be out of here tonight on the last freight."

Lynette clasped her hands together. "How exciting! I would love to do that."

He smiled and shook his head. "That's not a good idea, young lady. It's very dangerous. I only do it because it's the only way I can find work."

Lynette held out her hand. "Well, good luck. It was nice to meet you. My name is Lynette, by the way."

He took her hand and bowed slightly. "Toby Sinclair at your service."

A couple of young boys came up to the other end of the counter, nickels displayed for their attempt at riches. Toby straightened up and said, "I'd better get back to work. You girls have fun." He touched his hat and turned to the new customers. Edith grabbed Lynette's arm and pulled her away.

"Let's go, before you get in trouble," she said.

"Who, me?" Lynette fluttered her eyelashes.

"Yes, you," Bernie said. "'Please help little ol' me throw this heavy ring,'" she mimicked with an exaggerated southern accent.

"Oh, hush," Lynette said, slapping Bernie on the arm. She glanced over her shoulder to see if Toby overheard, but they were far enough away and he was busy with the two boys.

"Really, your ma would whip you if she was here," Edith said.

"Pooh, she doesn't know how to have fun. All she knows is work."

"She probably has to," Dinah said. Her impression of Lynette's mother was that there was very little money and it was all Florence Olsen could do to provide daily necessities for her family. Lynette seemed kind of lazy and self-absorbed.

"What do you know?" Lynette tossed her head and led the way to a hot dog stand. "Anyone hungry? I'll treat."

Dinah stood back. "I don't think so." She couldn't eat something that Lynette bought with money she had stolen from her poor mother.

"Suit yourself." Lynette was angry with the rest of them for criticizing her behavior. Edith accepted a hot dog but Bernie pulled a sandwich from the sack she had brought her clothes in. They sat on the ground under a tree to eat their supper and afterwards wandered around the sideshows again.

Soon Lynette produced a dainty yawn and said to Dinah, "Ready to go home?" Dinah looked at her in surprise and the other girls protested. It wasn't even dark yet.

"Sure. I guess," Dinah said.

As they headed home, Lynette said, "Ready for an adventure?"

"What?"

"I said, ready for an adventure? I'm going to hop that freight tonight."

"Don't do that! You heard what that guy said—it's dangerous. Lots of people get hurt."

"Lots of people don't. I'm sick of this town. Go to school and graduate and then what? Get married, have a bunch of kids and work yourself to death. I want to have some fun before I settle down."

"Why don't you go to college and get a job you like? Travel then."

Lynette stopped and looked at Dinah like she was stark raving mad. "Rich kids go to college. We're not rich. I'm going to do this and I want you to go with me."

"No, Lynette. I'm ready to go home, I think. I'll sleep in the camper tonight and tomorrow I'll be back where I belong."

"It's only for a couple of days and then we'll come back."

Dinah didn't believe her.

"Besides," she added, "if you don't come with me, I'll call the coppers and tell them about the trailer in our barn. Then how will you explain yourself?"

CHAPTER THIRTY-SIX
Dinah

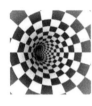 DINAH WAS SHOCKED. At first when she woke up this morning, she thought Lynette was a fun person she might want to spend several days with before she returned home. But as the day wore on, it seemed like Lynette became bossier and meaner.

"I—I don't want to."

"What are you, a fraidy-cat? We'll come back soon, I promise. You have to go with me."

Dinah walked in silence. What if Lynette did this and got hurt or killed? She would never have children, and Dinah, her mother, and her grandmother wouldn't exist. And even though she liked Lynette less than when they first met, she didn't want to see anything bad happen to her just on general principles.

"All right. I'll go."

Lynette ignored Dinah's lack of enthusiasm and said "Great! When we get home, go tie up a few clothes in a little bundle and bring your money. We may be able to pass some of it off. I'll meet you by the barn about 10:00. It'll be dark and the last freight goes through at 11:00. We'll have to get to the outside edge of town in case the bulls are watching by the station."

194

Dinah had a hundred questions but had the feeling Lynette would just make up answers. She went down the alley to the barn and quietly opened the door and slipped inside to the trailer. Once in, she sat on her bed to think. What if she locked herself in the trailer? If only she knew when the time change took place: right after she went to sleep, in the middle of the night or near morning?

If Lynette did call the police —and she wouldn't be surprised at that event—she wouldn't do it until after 10:00 and she found out Dinah wasn't going to join her. If Dinah could be asleep before then, maybe she and the trailer would already be gone. That plan might have the added benefit of delaying Lynette enough that she would be too late for the last freight.

Dinah changed into her jeans, a tee shirt and a black hoodie. Not appropriate for the time but she didn't plan to go back outside until she was home. From the bottom of her backpack, she pulled out some old sneakers and in doing so found a smashed bag of M & Ms, a real treasure considering that she didn't have any supper.

She wolfed those down, got up and locked the door, and lay back down, pulling a throw over her. In no time, she had dropped off, only to be awakened about ten minutes later by pounding on the door.

"Dinah! Dinah! Let me in!"

It was Lynette. Dinah looked at the little windup clock on the window sill. Only 8:45. What was she doing?

She got up and unlocked the door. "What?"

"C'mon. I think we should go sooner. There's a hobo camp on the edge of town and maybe somebody can help us get on that train. It's dark enough now." She looked at Dinah more closely. "Did you go to sleep?"

Dinah rubbed her eyes. "I guess." She couldn't think. What was she going to do?

Lynette barged in. "Got your stuff ready?" She scanned the trailer for Dinah's bundle.

"No, Lynette, I really don't think this is a good idea."

Lynette stomped her foot. "We're going, Dinah. C'mon."

Dinah thought a minute and remembered the importance of keeping Lynette safe and well for the future.

"Okay," she said, and put together a few things in her backsack.

Lynette led her through the alleys for a few blocks and then they followed the deserted streets to the rail yard. The last night of the fair undoubtedly drew a lot of people who might otherwise be out in their yards on a cool summer evening.

The rail yard presented a dark, threatening atmosphere, especially in contrast to the distant lights and sounds of the fair. It was not large but a few boxcars hulked in the darkness and a water tank loomed over the far end of the yard like a robot on stilts. Shadows added another degree of darkness. Dinah held on to the edge of Lynette's shirt but stumbled a couple of times anyway. They rounded the corner of a boxcar only a short distance from a man walking along the tracks swinging a large stick. He was silhouetted enough against a streetlight a half a block away that Dinah could see he wore some kind of uniform.

"Hey!" he yelled when he spotted them. "You kids get out of here!"

Lynette took off toward a nearby large shed and Dinah followed. She could hear the pounding footsteps following them. Behind the shed was a low fence that they climbed and sort of tumbled over to the other side.

"He won't chase us any farther. We're out of the rail yard," Lynette whispered. "C'mon."

She headed down a path through some scrubby trees. A few more blocks and they got to the edge of town. Dinah wrinkled her nose.

"What is that smell?"

"The dump. That's where the hobo camp is."

"Oh my God! Why would anybody put a camp there? That's awful."

"Watch your mouth, young lady." Lynette grinned. "My ma would wash it out with soap. They put it there because that's the only place they don't get chased out of. It's close to the railroad tracks and there's a little creek nearby where they can get water."

"How do you know so much about it?" Dinah said.

"Sometimes Edith and I sneak down here and just watch 'em. A couple of times we brought 'em leftovers from supper."

They rounded a bend and through the trees Dinah could see a couple of small fires.

As they got closer, she could make out a half dozen figures hunched over the fires. A couple were older, one was a teenaged boy and the others were men in their twenties or thirties. There were no women or girls. Several had on clothes that appeared to be too small or too big but all wore hats or caps. Their faces were dirty and they scratched at unseen pests. The firelight projected their shadows against the trees.

Dinah had a sudden recall of an incident from second grade. She had planned to be a bum for Halloween and described her plans in great detail to Grandma Linda. Her grandma looked at her sadly and said she really shouldn't make fun of "those people." Dinah didn't know what she meant because she didn't know at the time that hobos or bums actually existed. She thought her grandma was being silly, but decided to dress up as a nurse instead.

One of the older men looked up as they approached and frowned.

"Hey," Lynette said.

"Hey yourself. What are you girlies doin' here?"

"We're on the bum. Goin' to beat that last freight tonight," Lynette said matter-of-factly.

The man threw back his head and laughed. He looked at the others. "Hear that, boys? We got us a couple of tough girls here." He turned back to the girls. "You kids better git back home to your mommas. Scram!"

A red flush crept up Lynette's face, barely visible in the firelight. She crossed her arms. "Don't make fun of me."

The young boy sat on a log, arms around his knees and hands clasped. "Ooooh," he said softly and smirked.

Then he looked more closely at Lynette. "You brought us some noodles once."

Lynette nodded, and Dinah relaxed a little.

"I'm serious," the older man said. "You don't belong here. You got homes?"

Dinah started to nod, but Lynette jumped in. "No, my daddy threw me out. Lost his job, said he can't support me. No work here in town."

"That's for damn sure," mumbled one of the younger men.

"I'm goin' and you can't stop me," Lynette said.

"Just trying to make you see some sense. This isn't some romantic adventure, y'know."

"I know that. Just tell me this, where do you guys hop the train in this town?"

The older man just shook his head and stared down at his feet, but one of the younger ones said, "Back the direction you came from, edge of town near the water tank. They go pretty slow in there if they stop for water."

Dinah felt a stab of fear. Slow? The train wouldn't be stopped when they got on?

"I'm goin' tonight, I guess. Nothin' here for me. I'll show you." The boy got up.

"Hey, Sandy," one of the other men said. "You better treat those gals right."

Sandy waved him off. "'Course." Dinah assumed that Sandy got his name from his light ginger hair and freckles.

"Gotta clean up first," he said to the girls, and picked up a ragged satin bag and stuffed half a sandwich back in. He took the can he had been eating from down to the creek and rinsed it out. He left the can by the fire and picked up the bag.

"C'mon," he said, and they followed.

He walked ahead and said over his shoulder, "Old Dog's right, you know. If you have a home to go to, you should go there."

"Why do you call him Old Dog?" Dinah said.

"'Cause he hangs around here most the time and says he's too old to learn new tricks. But he knows all the old tricks and that's what's important when you're trying to survive."

Dinah looked at Lynette who shrugged and they trudged along the dirt street kicking up little puffs of dust. Feathery clouds scudded across the new moon creating moving shadows ahead of them. When they reached the tracks, they were a couple of blocks from the rail yard but Sandy turned along the tracks and continued a little farther out.

They sat down to wait on the ground.

"Where you from?" Lynette asked Sandy.

"Michigan. Detroit."

"Oh!" Dinah held up her right hand. "The mitten!"

"The what?"

She got flustered. That nickname must show up later. She had learned it from a friend at camp. "You know, Michigan's shaped like a hand…" She let it go because both Sandy and Lynette looked at her strangely.

A low rumble and vibration along the tracks preceded the mournful train whistle, different that the diesel horns she was used to. Even though several trains a day still go through town, Dinah had never paid much attention. This roaring monster spewing smoke and soot was a whole different can of worms, as her dad would say. And at that thought, the homesickness for her dad, mom, and Grandma Linda flooded her, blocking out the fear she felt at the approach of the train.

The train stopped for water and all she could see of it was the headlight.

THE ENGINE CHUGGED by, picking up speed. Over the noise, Sandy pointed at the open door of an approaching boxcar and yelled "That one!" He began running alongside the train and the girls followed. He reached up when the open door was alongside him and grabbed a handhold, just as hands reached out of the darkness to help him up. The girls did the same. Dinah found herself being partially lifted and partially dragged into the boxcar by a hand and the back waistband of her jeans.

"Getcher feet in!" someone was yelling and she snatched her feet back out of the opening. As the adrenalin rush subsided, she lay on the floor, feeling the metronome of the tracks under her back. She caught her breath and sat up. In the dark she could only make out shapes except for Lynette next to her and Sandy near the door.

"We did it!" Lynette said, leaning over to her. Dinah nodded, feeling the same exhilaration at their accomplishment in spite of her misgivings.

CHAPTER THIRTY-SEVEN

 IT WAS A LONG night. I woke up several times, checked my watch: 12:30, 1:24, 2:05, and so on. Each time I thought I would never get back to sleep and each time I was out immediately after thinking that. Finally it was 6:45. I got up as quietly as I could but realized it was still very dark. I peeked out the window and couldn't see a thing.

"Lynne?" Kurt's husky, early morning voice took me aback. I'd forgotten I wasn't alone, and that voice triggered a sudden loneliness.

"What time is it?" he asked, raising up on one elbow.

"Quarter to seven, according to my watch but it's so dark."

He sat up and checked out the back window. "Can't see anything," he said.

"I know." I opened the door. Gradually my eyes adjusted and I could see a rough wall straight ahead.

"Kurt, I think the trailer is inside a building."

He came up behind me and looked over my shoulder. When he didn't say anything, I turned around to face him. The shock on his face was epic.

"This can't happen," he said.

"I know, but it does." *I told you so* seemed a little over the top here — beating a dead horse, as it were.

Kurt pulled a pair of khakis on over his boxers and then a grey sweatshirt. It was a little warm for that but it didn't seem the time to discuss wardrobe. I stepped down out of the camper in my pajamas with the flashlight I kept over the door and Kurt followed. A workbench appeared in the faint beam and to one end, a door. I could see daylight around the edges.

Kurt reached around me and turned the doorknob, slowly pulling it open. Early morning light flooded in and we stood at the threshold of a bright world, feeling like we were on the cover of a fantasy book. The scene was familiar and it wasn't. I leaned out of the door and craned my head to the right.

There was my house, but instead of a sedate grey with crisp white trim, the siding was weathered with only scattered white blotches as evidence of its last paint job. There was no cozy screened porch and only rickety steps up to the back door. The vegetable garden was in the wrong place and there was no sign of my Heritage birch and two stately white pines in the back corner.

"Wow," said Kurt, looking around. "Your mom said there used to be a barn here. We're in it." He pinched himself and reacted with a gratifying pained expression.

"Now what?" he said.

"We dress appropriately and then see what we can find out about Dinah. I'm sure she's here."

He nodded, and we headed back to the trailer. Inside I donned one of my house dresses, a tiny green print with a little lace around the collar and the cuffs of the short sleeves. I pulled on my wedge sandals and perched primly on the edge of the dinette bed to watch Kurt fasten the tie he had brought—a nice wide brown-striped number —under the collar of a standard white dress shirt.

"Now roll your cuffs up," I instructed. As he did so, I noticed his digital watch. "Better put that in your pocket."

He set his hat, a find from Violet's that I had hung on a hook in the trailer for ambience, on his head at a jaunty angle and we returned to the side door of the barn. He peeked out, and once satisfied that no one was in sight, motioned me to follow quickly to the alley where we wouldn't be too visible from any of the homes on either side. We reached the sidewalk and slowed our pace.

"Do you have a plan?" he said.

I'd thought about it quite a bit but still wasn't real sure. "We walk down the street and case the joint?"

He grimaced. "Let me ask you this. If Dinah ended up here, are you sure she couldn't have also slept in the trailer last night and now be back in 2014?"

"I'm not sure about anything. But I think we tell the residents of my house that we are new in town and our daughter is missing. If she's there, or they have seen her, they have no reason not to tell us."

We rounded the corner onto our street, again familiar and yet not so much.

"Unless she has told them that she escaped from Bonnie and Clyde. You do kind of look like Bonnie—or at least Faye Dunaway. Except I think they're dead by now. But how do you know what date it is?"

I spotted a rolled up newspaper on the steps of the house we were passing and after checking for watchers, scooted up the sidewalk and picked it up. July 30, 1937.

"Ma'am, what are you doing? That's my paper." An old man stood in the open porch doorway of the house where Rene and John Gibson lived in 2014.

"Oh, sorry." I handed it to him. "I just saw the headline about Japan and wondered what had happened."

He snorted. "Attacked China, that's what. Heard it on the radio."

"Thank you," I said and backed down the sidewalk. "I wasn't going to take it—just look at the rest of the headline. Our son is in stationed in the Pacific and it's so worrisome."

"Gosh, that's okay," he relented. "We all need to know what's going on, don't we?" He gave a little wave to Kurt waiting on the sidewalk.

As we continued down the walk, Kurt said, "We have a son?"

"We do now. I meant to tell you."

"Well, that's great but I'll be happy if we can just find our daughter."

"Me too."

It was obvious that, just like in 2014, the side door was the one everyone used. The front door was closed tight while only the screen door was closed at the side. A small pot of zinnias, somewhat dried out by the summer heat, stood bravely on the steps trying to give a little welcome.

"Our name is Kelly, by the way," I whispered to Kurt as I raised my hand to knock.

A thin, weary looking woman came to the door wiping her hands on her apron. Her eyes were red and her brow was creased.

"Yes?" she said, looking very puzzled. She wasn't used to complete strangers at the door.

"Good morning," I said. "We're sorry to bother you so early but we just moved to town and our daughter Dinah has gone missing."

That startled her and her expression changed from puzzled to almost angry. But she nodded and held the door open. "Please come in."

We followed her up the couple of steps through the kitchen into the dining room. The kitchen startled me because of a lack of cupboards. A wall-hung sink was on one wall with a small Hoosier cabinet on another. A large wooden table stood in the center between the cabinet and a cookstove and provided the only workspace. The dining room seemed dim because of dark flowered wallpaper but I recognized the rectangular oak table.

A man in work clothes sat at the table, head in hands, a plate with a small helping of scrambled eggs and a piece of toast in front of him. He looked up.

"Robert, these people are the parents of the girl I told you about." She turned to us. "Dinah, right?"

I felt relief and at the same time concern. Something was wrong here.

"Yes," Kurt said. "Have you seen her?"

The woman abruptly turned to face us. "Oh, yes, we've seen her. She was here yesterday and apparently talked our Lynette into running away with her. Now they're both gone." Tears ran down her face unheeded.

"Flo," Robert said, and laid his hand on her arm, "Don't get yourself worked up again, honey."

"Gone?" I said, not able to process this. "Where?"

"We don't know of course," Flo said. "If we did, we wouldn't be so worried."

Robert looked at us. "Maybe you should leave."

"But if they are both missing, can't we work together to find them?" Kurt said. "When did you see them last?"

"They went to the fair yesterday afternoon with Edith and Bernie," Flo said. "I think Lynette was back sometime in the evening but I didn't see her."

"Then how did you know she was back?" I said.

Flo looked embarrassed. "I was listening to my program and I heard someone go up stairs and come back down but I didn't get up and see. She usually comes in and talks to me. But she must have gone back out."

"What about the friends they went to the fair with? Are they gone too?" Kurt said.

"We don't know yet. We haven't heard from their parents," Robert said.

I felt exasperated. "Can we contact them? Do you have their phone numbers?"

Robert shrugged. "We thought maybe she'd be back soon and no one would have to know she ran away."

Okay, so there was a pride thing going here. "What if we contacted them and just said we are looking for Dinah? At least we would know whether the other girls are gone too. And if not, maybe they know something. We won't mention Lynette."

Flo brightened. "I 'spose that would be all right. What do you think, Robert?"

He nodded, relieved, I think, to have the onus of bad parenting removed, at least publicly. He got up and got a pencil stub, pulled an used envelope out of the desk nearby and, after consulting the phone book, wrote on the back of it. He handed it to Kurt.

"Bernie Bedfield lives in the next block at this address. They don't have a telephone. Edith Schmidt's number and address is there." He pointed. "I think she's the one most likely to be in on this."

Flo wiped her hands again on her apron. "Will you let us know what you find out?"

"Certainly," I said. I led the way to the door. "I think we'll talk to Bernie first."

We were barely away from the house when Kurt said, "I can't wrap my head around this. That's our house — your house — so those people are…"

"You're right, my great-grandparents."

He looked up at the sky. "Wow."

"What time is it?" I asked.

He pulled his watch out of his pocket. "Almost 9:00."

"Okay. When we get there I think one of us needs to ask the questions and the other watch for body language."

"You ask the questions, especially if the girls are there. Besides, I might make some stupid slip. You have more experience at this."

"At being a time traveler, you mean?"

"I guess."

We stopped at the house number Robert had noted and Kurt said, "Chuck and Mindy's house."

"Right," I said, "but not yet."

We knocked on the door and waited. No answer, so Kurt knocked again. A tiny, slightly rounded girl with wavy brown hair and wire-rimmed glasses opened it.

"Hi," I said. "Might you be Bernie?"

She pushed the glasses up on her nose. "Bernice, yes."

"We're Mr. and Mrs. Kelly and we are looking for our daughter Dinah. Have you seen her?"

"Lynette's cousin? Not since last night."

"Did she talk about going somewhere else?"

"Nooo. I don't think so."

"Was she with anyone the last time you saw her?"

"Why, Lynette of course. They left the fair early — about 8:00, I think."

"Okay, thank you Bernie." I almost gave her my cell phone number in case she heard anything.

As we walked down the sidewalk, I said to Kurt, "Well, what did you think?"

"I think wherever Dinah is, she's with Lynette and that Bernie doesn't know anything else."

"That was my impression, too." I looked at the envelope Robert had given me. "Do you think we should call Edith's house first?"

209

"No. I'd rather see her face when we talk to her." He peered at the envelope in my hand. "She's on Webster Street, not far from downtown. I guess we're hoofing it."

"Unless you want to steal a bike."

"Better not." We picked up our pace and headed the five or six blocks to Edith Schmidt's house.

CHAPTER THIRTY-EIGHT

 EDITH LIVED IN an old Victorian close to the center of town. As we walked down the sidewalk, a red-headed girl came out of the front door with a cloth shopping bag and headed toward us. She looked about Dinah's age.

"Are you Edith Schmidt?" I asked.

She looked surprised and a little worried. "Why?" Natural instinct, I guess, before Stranger Danger became a preschool course.

I explained again about being Dinah's parents and that she was missing. She put her hand over her mouth and swallowed hard. "Is Lynette gone too?"

"Yes she is," Kurt said. "Do you know something about it? We're very worried about Dinah."

"Um, I don't know anything for sure, but Lynette always wanted to hop a freight. She said she wanted an adventure before she settled down." She shifted her eyes to the street and chewed the inside of her cheek.

"Do you think she really would have done that?"

She was almost in tears. "I don't know. I need to go the grocer's for my mom." She sidled around us and continued on her way. But then she stopped and turned back to us. "I know where you might be able to find out more."

"Where?" Kurt said, trying hard to keep his impatience in check.

"There's a hobo jungle south of the tracks, by the dump. We — Bernie and I — told her she was crazy and she wouldn't even know how to do it, but Lynette always said she could get help at the Jungle."

"Have you been there?" I asked her, wanting to shake her. I'd show her Stranger Danger.

She hung her head. "Once. Maybe twice. We took some food down to them."

"Can you show us?"

She shook her head. "I have to get stuff for my mom or she'll be mad. You can follow me downtown and I can tell you how to get there from there." She turned and trudged ahead.

Kurt looked at me and shrugged and we followed behind like a couple of puppies. When we reached Main Street, Edith stopped in front of the Corner Cash and Carry.

"I'm going here. If you go down this street about two blocks and then turn right and go to the edge of town, you'll see it. You'll smell the dump first."

As she gave us the directions, I remembered hearing from my dad about the old town dump in that location.

"I'm sure we can find it. Thank you for your help," I said.

"Can you let me know if you find them?" she asked.

"Certainly."

As we walked away, I explained more completely to Kurt the location of the dump. We found the little encampment nearby on the banks of the creek. There were only two men there on this bright morning. The older one looked at us curiously but said nothing. The other one ignored us.

Kurt explained our predicament. The man nodded. "I saw 'em last night. Tried to talk them out of it."

"Do you know if they actually did it?" I asked.

"Not for sure, but they went with Sandy. He was going to help them."

"What time did that train go through?"

"Eleven o'clock."

Kurt said "Thanks," and to me, "Let's check at the depot for the destinations."

I was starting to feel overwhelmed. We had lost her, tracked her, and lost her again. We walked back towards the center of town and turned toward the depot.

In 2014, the depot has been 'restored' and turned into a local history museum. Gleaming oak floors, edged by wainscoting and trim in a rich deep brown, are topped by smooth walls in a warm beige. There are no nicks or bubbles in any of the paint. All of the brass is polished and the window glass sparkles. It smells clean. It is a Disney version of the original depot. I volunteer as a host and guide once a month so I have spent quite a bit of time there just looking around.

But in 1937, the inside was like an old sepia photo. Shades of brown everywhere, but drab, flawed, and dusty.   Instead of an orderly display of railroad memorabilia encased in glass, battered benches filled the center of the waiting room in slightly crooked rows amidst scraps of paper on the floor. A wood stove sat cold and dark in the corner in deference to the summer heat. The windows were clouded with soot and dulled the bright sunshine.

An older man worked behind the ticket window. "Yes?" A northeastern twang to his voice.

Kurt put his hands on the little ledge of the ticket window, pulled them back and dusted them off, put them in his pockets. "Can you tell us the destination of the train that came through here at eleven o'clock last night?" I bent to pick up a couple of pieces of paper near my feet.

"San Francisco." He stamped papers on the counter in front of him with a large date stamp producing a rhythmic pattern of ka-womps. At his words, my head jerked up and my heart fell.

"It doesn't stop before then?" Kurt said.

The old man looked at him more closely. "'Course it does. The final destination is San Francisco."

I touched the greasy surface of an oil lantern sitting by the window. It was — or certainly looked like — the one in a glass case hanging on the wall in 2014 right above the table where museum visitors signed in.

"So where is the next stop?"

"Grinnell, Des Moines, Omaha..."

Kurt put one hand on his hip and ran the other through his hair. "Okay. Thanks," he said and motioned me outside.

"This is hopeless," he said. "Those girls, if they got on last night, could get off anywhere."

"We need to talk to Robert and Flo."

"Your great-grandparents."

"My great-grandparents."

"It's very odd," he said.

"Tell me about it."

We took the most direct route we could back to their house. My house. My mother's old house. Whatever.

Flo was just walking up from the back yard with a basket of onions and cabbage at her hip.

"Did you find out anything?" She had one hand resting on her throat.

"Maybe," Kurt said. "Is your husband here?"

She nodded and held the door open.

This time she invited us to sit at the table—our table—and offered us coffee. We declined and she took a chair across from me. Kurt described our visits with Bernie and Edith. When he got to the part about the hobo jungle and the girls hopping the freight, Flo gasped and turned quite pale.

"She wouldn't do that! Not Lynette."

Robert leaned forward and took her hand. "Yes, she would, Flo. That girl has a wild streak that you refuse to see," he said quietly.

"The point is not who's to blame," I said. "The point is that as far as we know, our daughters left town last night on a westbound train and we don't know whether they are still on it, or if they got off somewhere along the way. Do you have any ideas?"

CHAPTER THIRTY-NINE
Dinah

 DINAH SAT UP and looked around the boxcar but the murky darkness made it impossible to distinguish anything more than vague shapes. She clutched her little backsack to her chest. Lynette crawled over to her.

"Are you okay?"

"Yeah. Lynette, where are we going?"

"West, I think."

"West? That's half the country." She found it difficult to keep her balance even sitting down with the rocking of the car.

Lynette giggled. "I wonder if that ring toss guy is in here."

"He'd probably throw you off for being so dumb."

"Hey," Lynette whispered, "if you *are* my great-granddaughter, I must survive this, right? So I'm invincible."

"Better get some sleep, girls." It was Sandy, behind them. Dinah realized then that the rest of the car was quiet except for a couple of subdued voices barely heard over the clacking of the car on the rails.

She tried to get comfortable on the floor of the boxcar, using her little backsack as a pillow. Lynette curled up against her, back to back. But sleep eluded her. What if something happened to the trailer while she was gone? Someone was bound to find it sooner or later. She hadn't thought this through — at any point. She had believed she would be in control — if she wanted to go back, she could do it at any time. But she hadn't really *thought*.

Lynette saw this as a lark with no consequences. Dinah had to convince her otherwise before circumstances did. She finally slept. She dreamed she was running a little restaurant and all of her family was there helping cook and wash dishes but no one would wait on tables.

WHEN SHE WOKE, faint light was coming in the open box car door. Fields of tall corn confined by fences zipped by outside. She sat up, hugged her knees, and watched the panorama glide by, wondering what this day would bring. She was thirsty and needed a bathroom. More lack of forethought.

A rustling off to her left produced a person from a shapeless mass. A young man emerged from his cocoon but still needed a lot of transformation. He needed a shave, looked dirty, and wasn't eager to see the day.

"Good morning," Dinah said.

"Not much good about it." He yawned and stretched and a waft of bad breath hit her in the face. To be fair, she was sure hers was the same.

"What are you doing on here?" he asked.

Good question. She shrugged. "I honestly don't know. Watching out for my friend, I guess." She indicated Lynette. "How about you?"

He pushed his hair out of his eyes. "It was either leave home or probably off my old man. Got tired of getting pushed around and beat up." He turned away from her.

"I'm sorry."

He turned back. "Most of the guys on here either had to leave to find work or else are trying to get away from a bad situation. Like me. A few think they're going to find a big adventure." He stared at her and she knew which group he had put her in.

"It's not like that...," she started to say but Lynette was stirring. She sat up and looked around.

"Where are we?"

Dinah was completely exasperated with her. "On a train. It was your dumb idea."

"Oh, yeah!" Lynette grinned. "Have we stopped anywhere?'

Dinah looked at the guy she'd been talking to. "I don't know. Have we?"

He laughed but he wasn't amused. "Yeah. We're almost to Des Moines."

"Des Moines?" Dinah was shocked but that was dumb. They'd been on the train all night; where did she think they would end up? Twenty miles down the line?

Instead of rows and rows of corn passing outside the door, factories, many run down and vacant, began appearing. A hazy smoke hung over many of the buildings. Metal on metal screeched as the train slowed, the box car jerked several times, and everyone in the car was moving, gathering up bags, shoes, and even a pan or two.

"What's happening?" Dinah asked.

"Big yard like this, the bulls will be along checking every car." He tied up his bundle and went to the door. As soon as the train had slowed, he swung out and landed on his feet. Others left the same way and scattered. Lynette and Dinah waited until the train had almost stopped before trying it. Lynette landed on her feet but Dinah stumbled and went face first in the cinders. She caught herself with her hands but pain exploded in her palms from the sharp rocks.

Lynette reached down and grabbed her arm and tried to haul her up.

"C'mon, there's a bull coming!"

Dinah got her feet under her and stole a quick glance behind her. A large man with a muscular torso but only one arm pounded toward them along the stopped train. His remaining arm wielded a huge club, circling it in the air like a lariat. He seemed focused on the two girls when a man emerged from the rods under the boxcar only a few feet in front of him.

The bull let loose a roar befitting his epithet and brought the club down on the man's head with such force that Dinah started back to help.

"No!" Lynette still had hold of her arm and pulled her away.

"He's going to kill that guy," Dinah shouted.

"If we go back, he'll kill us," Lynette said.

Dinah started to cry, and let Lynette drag her, but kept looking back at the horror taking place behind them.

They ran, not stopping until they reached the edge of the rail yard. By then, Dinah was sobbing, desperately needing a bathroom, and regretting ever deciding to time travel on her own.

"There's a filling station." Lynette pointed across the street. "We can use their bathroom."

After brushing her teeth, combing her hair and washing her face, Dinah felt a little better. She tied her hoodie around her waist to accommodate the increasing heat. Her outfit would probably draw attention but she couldn't help that.

"Now what?"

"There's a diner over there. Let's get something to eat and we can think about it," Lynette said.

"If I think about it, I'll go home," Dinah said.

"Oh, come on. It's exciting."

"Watching a man get beat to death? Really, Lynette?" Dinah left Lynette standing and headed for the diner. She walked in and took a seat at the counter. Lynette followed her and slid on to the stool next to her.

"Are you mad at me?"

Dinah was too disgusted to answer. She could tell by Lynette's wheedling tone that she often used it to get her way.

"You're supposed to be nice to your great-grandma," Lynette whispered and giggled at Dinah's discomfort.

Dinah relented and they looked over the menu to see what they could afford. They finally decided to split a breakfast that included two fried eggs and two pieces of toast for a quarter. When Lynette ordered, she asked the waitress, a gaunt, crabby woman, for an extra plate and fork.

"Not for that price, honey. You're already taking up two stools for the price of one meal." She stuck her pencil behind her ear and left to turn in their order.

Dinah was embarrassed by the whole situation and ducked her head.

"What a hag," Lynette said.

"Shush, people are looking at us," Dinah said.

"Who cares?"

But when the waitress returned, she set two plates on the counter in front of them. Each contained two eggs, toast and even a couple of anemic-looking strips of bacon.

Dinah looked up at the waitress in surprise. "But…"

"Don't worry about it, honey. Those guys took pity on you and paid your bill." She nodded toward two men at the end of the counter.

One wore overalls and a grey newsboy cap. His round open face seemed almost childlike as he smiled at the offerings on the menu. The other was older and wore pants with suspenders over a rumpled grey shirt, with a battered straw hat pushed back on his head. He saw the girls looking at them and touched a finger to the brim of his hat and nodded. There were a couple of teeth missing in his smile.

Dinah gave a little smile and mouthed 'thank you.' Lynette was already digging in, dipping her toast in the egg yolk between bites of bacon. Dinah thought it was probably the best meal she'd ever had. They were just about finished when the men pushed away their plates and got up to leave.

As they passed the girls, the older one said, "You girls get enough to eat?"

"Yes, thank you," Dinah said.

"Are you travelin'?"

"Yup," Lynette said. "Headin' west. We've been riding the rails." She made it sound like their experience was counted in months rather than hours.

"Bert's got a car," the younger man said proudly. "We're driving to California, aren't we, Bert?" He wagged his head at his friend.

Bert ignored him. "You girls be careful. The rails are dangerous for anyone but especially young folks like you." He touched his hat again and off they went.

A slow smile leaked over Lynette's face. One that Dinah had come to be wary of over the last twenty-four hours. She slid off her stool and picked up her bag off the floor.

"C'mon."

Dinah followed her out. "What have you cooked up now?"

Lynette didn't answer but made a beeline for an old black car, boxy and faded, looking to Dinah like something out of an old gangster movie. The two men were just opening the doors.

"Wait!" Lynette called and broke into a run. Bert turned and smiled. "What's the problem?" he said when they reached the car.

"If you're going to California, could you give us a ride, maybe just to the next town?" Lynette said. "There's a bull in this rail yard who was after us."

Dinah grabbed her arm. "Lynette…"

"Well," said Bert, and Dinah caught a wink when he looked at his companion. "You don't even know us and…"

"We know you better than we know anyone else here," Lynette said. "Please?"

Burt rubbed his head. "I suppose it would be okay. Get in the back."

Dinah felt like she was on a sled hurtling downhill totally out of control. She got into the back seat as instructed but pinched Lynette on the leg as they got seated.

"Ow!" Lynette said and gave her a look to kill. Dinah felt miserable. She looked around for a seat belt and then realized she wasn't going to find one.

Bert said over his shoulder, "We have to make a stop first at our hotel to pick up our stuff, okay?"

"Sure," Lynette said, still glaring at Dinah. "We really appreciate it."

Bert drove a couple of blocks and pulled up in front of a disreputable looking building. He and his friend got out.

"We'll just be a few minutes. Do you want to wait in the car or come with us?"

"We'll wait," Dinah said firmly.

When the men had gone inside, Dinah said, "Lynette, this is a bad idea."

Lynette turned and stared out the window.

Dinah dug in her backsack for her little coin purse. She unzipped it and pulled out a few bills and some coins.

"Some of this money would pass I bet, and we could get a ticket on a passenger train so no one could bother us." Several of the coins slipped out of her hand and rolled down the grey scratchy seat into the crack.

"Oh no," she said.

"Good move," Lynette said. "You're more trouble than you're worth."

Dinah stuck her hand down in the crack and felt for the change. She touched a piece of cloth—probably a rag or something—maybe the coins got caught in it. She pulled it out and held it up.

And immediately dropped it. The pink cloth was stained with large reddish-brown spots that looked suspiciously like dried blood. Lynette turned and looked at the cloth.

"What is it?" She picked it up and held it out. It wasn't a rag; it was a girl's blouse.

Dinah clutched at her bag and stared. "Lynette, we need to get out of here now!"

She opened her door as Lynette said, "Maybe there's a reasonable explanation…"

"I'm not waiting to find out, and if you have a brain in your head, you won't either." She slammed her door and started to run down the street away from the direction they had come. Lynette's door slammed too and Dinah could hear footsteps behind her.

They had reached the end of the block when they heard Bert shout. "Girls! Come back!" The car engine started. Dinah ducked into a narrow alley filled with garbage cans. Too late she realized it was a dead end.

"Behind this trash." She pulled Lynette down behind some cans and barrels. The smell was overpowering and the flies relentless. She peeked up above the cans in time to see the old black car pass slowly by the alley entrance. At least she thought it was the same car. It seemed like all of the cars she had seen were black and boxy.

They waited a few minutes. When it didn't come back and no other similar cars passed, Dinah said, "Let's go the other way. Maybe we can get back to that diner."

To her surprise, Lynette followed without argument. At the alley opening, Dinah looked both ways. Traffic was light and very few people were on the streets.

"Run!" Dinah said and took off toward the hotel, and beyond that in a couple of blocks, the diner. As they passed on the opposite side of the street from the hotel, Dinah felt a gripping chill in spite of the heat when she spotted what she thought was the car sitting on a side street. She grabbed Lynette's hand and yelled, "Faster!" As they passed the corner, she heard the car start up. Since she had quit soccer the spring before, Dinah hadn't done much running, a lapse she now regretted. Her chest was starting to hurt and Lynette was gasping for breath too.

"Through there." Lynette pointed to stacks of crates next to a small shop. They ducked through the rows and came out behind the stacks by a warehouse. They stopped and bent over, hands on knees, to catch their breath.

"Well, girlies, you're back."

Dinah stood up and looked into the face of the one-armed railroad bull.

CHAPTER FORTY

THE ATMOSPHERE IN Flo and Robert's dining room was as dark as the decor. In 2014, it would be enough of a shock to know that Dinah could be anywhere from the middle of the country to the West Coast. With 1937 communications and transportation, the prospect was a bottomless chasm. We had no car and of course our phones wouldn't work. I hadn't noticed a telephone in the house.

"Do you have a car?" I asked.

Robert shook his head. "We had to sell it."

A banging commenced on the side door, followed by a shout.

"Flo!"

Flo looked apologetic. "It's my brother, Archie."

I had heard of Great-Great Uncle Archie from my mother. His escapades were part of the family lore. Of course, it wouldn't be wise to mention that—or that he would be lost at the Battle of the Bulge.

Archie let himself in, bounded up the steps, and presented himself in the dining room, cap in hand.

"Oh, excuse me. I didn't know you had company. I need to talk to you and Robert privately. It's really important." He shifted from one foot to the other.

"We'll step outside," Kurt said, and I followed him out.

A fairly new truck was parked in the driveway.

"Must be Archie's," I said. "He had a little more money than the rest of the family because he married money. Not much but more than most people in these times."

Kurt interlaced his fingers behind his neck and stretched, his elbows almost like wings. He put his hands back in his pockets and gazed up at the tree tops.

"I still can't get my head around this. How can we be in two different times? I mean, neither of us is born yet so how can we be here? And how on earth are we going to find her with no car—"

Flo opened the door. Her face was tear-streaked but more relaxed. "Can you come back in? This is about the girls."

We hurried back up the half-flight of steps, through the kitchen, and into the dining room. Archie, who had pretty much ignored us when he first came in, now looked at us with new interest.

Flo turned back to us. "The girls are in jail. In Des Moines."

Kurt looked stunned. "Jail? "What for?"

"They were arrested for vagrancy at the rail yard," Robert said. "Lynette called Archie because we don't have a phone."

I felt a little sob well up and I turned to hug Kurt. 'In jail' wasn't great but at least now we knew where she was.

"She was crying, poor thing. She sounds pretty scared," Archie said.

Robert scoffed. "She *should* be scared. But that girl can turn the tears on anytime she wants."

"Oh, Robert, don't be so mean. I'm sure she is scared and regretting every minute of this," Flo said.

"It's you that has spoiled her, woman. But I'd best go get them. Can I borrow your truck, Arch?"

"Why don't you stay here with Flo and I'll get 'em. I got directions up here." He pointed at his head.

"What can we do? Give you some money?" Kurt reached for his billfold. I wasn't sure what he was going to pull out of it that wouldn't cause problems.

"No, I'll take care of it and you can pay me back."

AFTER ARCHIE LEFT, Kurt and I excused ourselves to go "home" for a little bit and said we would be back in a few hours. As we got away from the house, I said, "What are we going to do about money?"

He touched the gold locket at my neck. "We're going to try and find a pawn shop."

Relief flooded through me. "Great idea!" I unhooked the locket and put it in his hand. "Do you suppose there is one in town? There isn't in our time."

"I know but I think they were more common in the Depression. We'll go downtown and ask."

As we walked downtown, I said, "Gives you a different perspective on town, walking everywhere, doesn't it?"

He chuckled. "I was just thinking the same thing."

We stopped at Swan's Drugstore because it looked like the most likely source of local information. Kurt had enough change that he had stolen from his coin collection to get us each a cup of coffee. The waitress was pleasant but no nonsense; you had the feeling she could command a battalion or a church supper if necessary.

When she set the thick white mugs of coffee in front of us, Kurt said, "We're just passing through town. Is there a pawn shop here?"

She put down the rag she had been using to shine the chrome of the soda fountain fixtures. "Not as such. But Davy Digman has a little place around the corner where he fixes radios and he does a little pawn brokering on the side."

Kurt thanked her and she moved down the counter to exchange observations on the weather and the baseball season with other customers. We sipped our coffee silently, listening to the chatter around us. With our cups still half full, we looked at each other, eager to complete another step in getting our daughter back.

"Ready?" he said.

"Let's do it."

We found Davy Digman's shop and stepped inside to what must have seemed quaint and outdated even to 1937ites. A wood floor coated with decades of grease and dirt; a desk piled with tubes and broken radios, and a couple of glass cases displaying guns, jewelry, watches and glassware. Bare light bulbs hung from the ceiling by wires that would meet no safety standards in any time period. A short man wearing an eye shade emerged from a back room carrying a small box of junk.

"Afternoon," he said. "What can I do for you?"

Kurt showed him the necklace and asked him what he would loan us on it.

Davy took it and held it under a small lamp. He opened the locket—it was empty— and turned it over and examined the back side.

"Ten bucks. You have thirty days to retrieve it."

"It's a deal," Kurt said, and soon we were on our way back toward the Olsen's house. We turned at the corner before the house and followed the alley to the old barn. Once back inside the trailer, we collapsed on the still open beds, relieved to have a few minutes when we didn't have to worry about committing some faux pas and drawing unwanted attention.

Kurt pulled his watch out of his pocket. "If all goes well, Archie could be back with the girls in a couple of hours. Maybe we should try and rest a little."

I agreed, and lay down with my book. I couldn't sleep though. Thoughts raced through my head of all the things that could still go wrong. I was glad to hear soft snores from Kurt. He had had a lot to take in during the last twenty-four hours.

I checked my little alarm clock about every five minutes and finally an hour and a half had passed. I shook Kurt gently and his eyes shot open. He looked around, groping for a point of reference.

"It's 3:00," I said. "Archie could be back with the girls pretty soon."

"Right." He sat up and rubbed his eyes. "I don't know about you but I'm ready for this to be over."

"Me, too. At first, Dinah and I were intrigued with just being observers of a previous time. So different from the static pictures or even movies that you see. But I think it's pretty hard to do that."

We straightened our clothes and the bed; then walked around the barn and through the alley so we could come up the front walk to the Olsens'. Flo and Robert sat on a rickety porch swing on the open front porch that no longer existed.

"Have you heard anything?" I asked as we walked up the front walk.

They both looked at me funny. "We don't have a telephone," Robert reminded me.

"I'm sorry. Us either. I don't know what I was thinking." We sat down on the steps.

"So Mr. Kelly, what do you do?" Robert asked.

Kurt leaned back against the railing so he could look at Robert. What would be Robert's reaction if he said 'computer programmer'?

"I've been working in a bank but it closed. So I'm looking for an accountant position."

Robert nodded. "Just got to find a business that's makin' enough money that they can pay someone to keep track of it."

"You are so right," Kurt said. "So meanwhile, I'll probably take anything I can find. My brother lives in St. Louis and he says he can get me a job where he works. So we'll probably be moving on."

"I wish you well. There's a lot of good men looking."

"Who do you follow in baseball?" Kurt asked, and for a half hour managed to steer Robert into a near monologue on his favorite team, the Chicago White Sox. I asked Flo to show me her garden and we talked about tomatoes, beans, and canning methods. We also talked about the challenges of fourteen-year-old girls and the best way to get clothes white. Flo shared how she could stretch a small piece of ham for three meals.

Finally we heard Archie's truck pull into the drive. We came around the corner of the house just as Dinah alighted from the truck and saw me.

"Mom!" She ran and threw her arms around me.

She finally let go and pulled back, and then glimpsed Kurt who had come up behind me.

"Daddy!" Even more exuberance. I had long ago accepted that he would always be her favorite.

She looked at both of us. "I'm so sorry. We were really scared. This bull—like, he's a guard and this guy had one arm and we saw him beat a man earlier and we were running from some other guys and ran right into him. He would have beat us too with this big club he carries but another guard came by and arrested us and had the police pick us up. I didn't know how we were going to get back." She took a breath.

I glance over at Lynette and her parents. Lynette, who could have easily been Dinah's sister, was sobbing, I thought a little dramatically.

"I didn't want to go," she was saying. "Dinah thought it would be fun…"

Dinah heard the last part and silently shook her head at us. But she said "I'm sorry, Lynette. It was a big mistake." And to Archie, "Thank you for coming to get us."

"Yes," Kurt said to him and pulled out his billfold. "How much was the bail?"

Archie shook his head. "They let them go with a warning. Told them not to come back to Des Moines until they were twenty-one." He grinned.

Kurt handed him a five from Davy Digman's shop. "Here take this for gas and your trouble."

Archie protested that it was too much but Kurt insisted. I had the feeling from looks that were exchanged that Archie might share this windfall with his sister.

I WAS ANXIOUS to get away. These ancestors of mine seemed like a pretty dysfunctional bunch — Robert beaten down by economic necessities, Flo by hard work and not much hope, and Lynette manipulating them both. We didn't have the full story yet but I trusted Dinah. She was usually honest with us, as I felt now that she had been about the young man in the library.

"We should be going," I said.

"Yes," Kurt said. "Thank you all for your help. We really didn't know where to turn."

Flo relaxed a little and smiled at us. "It was nice to meet you, in spite of everything." She could afford to be magnanimous now that she believed her daughter had been led astray by the evil Dinah. She cocked her head and looked at me. "You do look familiar…"

I laughed. "Well, you know, they say everyone has a double."

We said our goodbyes and, turning down an offer of a ride from Archie, headed down the sidewalk. Kurt suggested we use our remaining cash for a supper downtown, partly because we all needed a full meal and partly because it would kill some time before we could go to sleep in the trailer.

CHAPTER FORTY-ONE

ON THE WAY downtown, Dinah told us her side of the story.

"Mom, I was so worried that something would happen to Lynette, and then Grandma Linda, you and me would never be born. I had to go along with her. But she's kind of crazy."

Kurt smiled at me over Dinah's head.

"It happens," I said.

We reached a small restaurant, and seated ourselves in a booth. The five dollars we had left was more than enough for the blue plate special for each of us—fried chicken, mashed potatoes with gravy and fresh corn off the cob. Dinah's description of their encounter with the two men was especially frightening. It wasn't that Dinah was safer in our own time. It was just that we had more resources. Something had to be done about the trailer when we returned,

"Mom, I've been thinking about Ben. Do you think he time traveled in the trailer?"

"I've wondered, but I don't know. Why?"

She sopped up some gravy with her roll. "He told you 'I took her back', right?"

"Yes."

"What if he went back to see Minnie before they broke up and tried to change things?"

"I don't know if you can change history," Kurt said.

I was taken with Dinah's idea.

"She might be still alive," I said. "I think I'll check it out when we get back."

"How are you going to do that?" Kurt said.

"Ben told me her maiden name, if I can just remember it. I ought to be able to find marriage or death records, maybe property taxes."

Dinah talked almost nonstop while we finished our meal and walked back toward the Olsens'. She speculated about Ben and Minnie, described how different life was in the Thirties than our own time, and expounded on Lynette's behavior, which she thought was rude and inconsiderate to her parents and her friends. Interesting.

We took the alley route to the barn, and making sure no one was watching, went in the side door. Once in the trailer, Kurt locked the door. The battery was running low for the lights so we sat in the dark, quietly talking about all of our experiences. When the lighted dial on Kurt's watch said 8:30, we lay down on the beds, Kurt on the couch and Dinah and I on the dinette bed.

Every once in awhile, one of us would say softly, "Everyone still awake?" We all were. Finally I could hear Dinah's breathing slow and even out, and not much longer after that Kurt's rhythmic snoring. I don't remember much after that.

MY FIRST CLUE that we were no longer in the barn was grey light filtering through the curtains. I was clinging to the edge of the narrow bed and I rolled off to the floor and sat hugging my knees. I could hear Dinah breathing behind me and see Kurt's form on the other bed, so I sat for a few moments savoring what I hoped was our return to where we belonged. I decided I'd better check for sure.

I unlocked the door and peeked outside. My garden, my porch, my house.

"Wake up, sleepyheads! We're back!"

They took their time, moaning and groaning. Finally the change sunk in and they each hastily gathered their things. It was like Christmas morning.

"Has your dad shown you how good he is at cooking breakfast?"

Dinah said, "I'm the one who taught him," and they high-fived each other.

I tweaked Dinah's cheek. "C'mon. Your grandma's been waiting I'm sure very impatiently. We'd better get in and assure her you are okay."

"Don't get sappy, Mom."

"Ha! You were a little sappy yourself yesterday when you got out of that truck," Kurt said, and she stuck out her tongue at him. Now if she'd just throw a tantrum, I would be sure she was fine.

We trooped into the house and met my mother in the kitchen who had heard all of the commotion.

"Oh, Dinah!" she squealed and they hugged each other, actually jumping up and down like a couple of teenagers from the cast of *Grease*. I didn't know my mother could jump.

Kurt took the earlier hint and shooed us out of the kitchen so he could cook breakfast. Since my mother had been there for twenty-four hours, I was sure the refrigerator was well stocked.

Dinah and I sat at the dining room table and related our adventures to Mom. She shook her head regretfully at Lynette's part in the drama.

She covered Dinah's hand with her own. "I'm sorry honey. She wasn't like that as my mother, but I heard stories. She was a pretty rebellious young lady."

Dinah cocked her head at her grandma. "Did you ever get in trouble when you were my age, Grandma Linda?"

I perked up. "Yes, tell us, Mother."

"Well, let's just say I wasn't a perfect angel."

"Nobody is, I guess," Dinah said. "It's just that you hear people say 'In my day...' like this generation is the only one with problems."

"You're right," Mom said. "We older folks tend to forget our youth and get a little judgmental, I guess."

Dinah grinned. "So you had fun, too."

"We did. I'll tell you about it sometime when your parents aren't listening."

Kurt brought in a platter of pancakes and sausage. I got out plates and silverware and we dug in.

I put down my fork. "We need to call the police. What are we going to tell them?"

"You called the police?" Dinah was back to being appalled by her parents' behavior.

"Of course we did," Kurt said. "We checked with your friends and had no idea where you were. We didn't think about the trailer until the end of the day, and naturally I didn't believe your mom about the time travel."

"Oh. My. God. What will everyone think? Did they do one of those alerts?"

"Yes, they did. What did you expect, Dinah? We were frantic," I said.

"We were afraid at first that you had been abducted. You were seen talking to an older boy at the library and no one knew much about him," Kurt added.

"Oh, no." Dinah put her face in her hands.

"So we need to come up with a plausible story. Obviously no one will believe the real one," I said.

She pushed back from the table and started to get up, her face red with anger.

"Dinah, sit down," Kurt said firmly, surprising us all. He was not usually the disciplinarian. "None of this would have happened if you hadn't gotten mad before and disappeared."

She looked at her grandmother for help, got a shrug, and returned to her chair.

"Maybe we could say I was at camp," she said, head down.

"Right," said Kurt. "And your parents just forgot that they took you there?"

She shrugged. "We could say I was abducted and I got away."

"Then the police would waste time and manpower continuing a search. Plus you would have to undergo a physical exam at the hospital," I said. That stopped that plan.

"I think you need to say that you just ran away and saw the Amber Alert so you came back home," Kurt said. "Otherwise someone else will get dragged into it. Lynne, why don't you call Officer Muller while Dinah and I work out enough details to make her story believable."

So that's what we did. Dinah had to endure a lecture from Muller about what she had put her parents through, but the police decided to drop the investigation.

CHAPTER FORTY-TWO

LIFE RETURNED TO some semblance of normal. Dinah spent most of her time at home so that she didn't have to answer embarrassing questions. She didn't go to the library at all, but spent a lot of time writing in her diary. She did visit Ben several times, and most days he was up for a game of cribbage.

I worked from home whenever possible and mulled over the plan to make the trailer into an office. Meanwhile, I kept it locked and the key on a chain around my neck. After wracking my brain, I finally came up with Minnie's last name—Gunder. I did several online searches and found a marriage record in 1956 to a Harold Batterson. Tax records showed that they owned property in Davenport. A search for Harold turned up an obituary from five years earlier, but I didn't find one for Minnie.

So I wrote a letter to Minnie, addressing it to the last property address. I explained how I knew Ben and told her that I wanted to let her know about his stroke and current condition. That was in August, and there was no response.

School started again and Dinah buried herself in activities. The trailer remained locked and began to look like it had when it sat behind Ben's barn. On the Saturday before Halloween, Dinah had volunteered to help with a corn maze sponsored by the local Lion's Club. We made pumpkin cookies to sell and I helped take tickets at the gate. The afternoon was a huge success — one of those crisp fall days when the sky was so blue that it almost hurt your eyes. We had a few cookies left so when I dropped Dinah off at home, I put the cookies on a plate and took them to Ben. He was sitting in an arm chair with a football game on the TV when I got there but was mainly staring out the window.

He perked up, as he always did when he saw me.

"Oh, I love anything pumpkin," he said, when he saw the cookies and immediately took two.

I described the corn maze and he chuckled at the little stories I told him about the kids. I was just getting ready to leave when there was a soft knock at the door.

A petite woman with her grey hair back combed into a bouffant hairdo and a matching green jacket and knit pants stood in the doorway. She had the same bright blue eyes I had met on the beach. Ben looked at her for a moment and then broke into the widest smile I have ever seen on anyone.

"Minnie!" he said, and held out his hand.

She came forward and took it. "Ben, you old reprobate. What are you doing in here?"

"Waiting for you," he said, and the tears began to track down his face.

I introduced myself, and then said I'd better go.

"But before I do, Ben, I want you to tell me about that trailer." I plunged ahead. "You know it time travels, right?"

Ben looked like the proverbial cat with the canary, and then said with great innocence, "What happened?"

I waved that off. "I'll tell you all about it later. Did it always time travel?"

Ben shook his head. "No, it got hit by lightning one night and we thought that did it."

"So did you go back to try and patch things up with Minnie so you could marry her?"

"Oh, no," Minnie said. "We did get married before that. After the accident, the doctors didn't think I would last very long because of my injuries. Ben took me back and broke up with me. At the time I thought he didn't want all of the work of taking care of an invalid. But over the years, I came to realize that he believed if I was with someone else, I would avoid the accident and live a full life." She smiled at Ben. "Harold was a good man and a devoted husband, but I don't think anyone ever loved me like Ben."

I was confused. "But, when I was looking for you, I found a marriage recorded to Harold but not to Ben."

"When we returned to 1954, it erased all of that. We reverted to the ages we had been then but still knew what happened later. I begged Ben not to leave me, but now I know why he did."

"So that's why no one remembers you being married," I said to Ben. The truth dawned on me. "Ben, you are a reprobate! You sold me that trailer and hoped I would find Minnie somewhere along the way. You were afraid going back would somehow result in the accident again."

He grinned. "Well, I thought you'd have fun with it along the way, too. It's pretty exciting, right?"

"Hah! More exciting than you know. You should have told me."

"Would you have believed me?"

I had to concede. "I'll leave you two to catch up. Some rainy day when you're bored, I'll tell you everything that's happened to that trailer this summer."

I said good-bye and left but I don't think they noticed. I left overjoyed at Ben's reunion with Minnie, but angry at all the fear and grief his little game had caused. When I got home, I told Dinah about Minnie.

"Oh, what a wonderful story. I wish I had gone along and met her."

I put my arm around her shoulders. "I think you are probably going to get that chance."

TRAILER ON THE FLY

Follow Lynne McBriar's further adventures when the Time Travel Trailer meets the Sisters on the Fly in *Trailer on the Fly.*

How many of us have wished at some time or other we could go back in time and change an action or a decision or just take back something that was said? But it is what it is. There is no rewind, reboot, delete key or any other trick to change the past, right?

Lynne McBriar can. She bought a 1937 camper that turned out to be a time portal. And when she meets a young woman who suffers from serious depression over the loss of a close friend ten years earlier, she has the power to do something about it. And there is no reason not to use that power.

Right?

Available from Amazon in paper back, ebook and in audible version.

THANK YOU

For taking your time to share the time travel trailer's adventures. Just as the sound of a tree falling in the forest depends on hearers, a book only matters if it has readers. Please consider sharing your thoughts with other readers in a review on Amazon or emailing me at karen.musser.nortman@gmail.com. My website at www.karenmussernortman.com provides updates on my books, my blog, and photos of our for-real camping trips.

You can get a free copy of the first Frannie Shoemaker Campground Mystery, *BATS AND BONES*, if you sign up for my Favorite Readers email list to receive occasional notices about my new books and special offers.

Go to this link:
www.karenmussernortman.com

Acknowledgments

This has been fun. As a former history teacher, I enjoyed exploring past decades in a little more detail, looking at hairstyles, clothing, lists of popular songs and such. Lynne and Dinah's darker experiences are also based in fact. Prisoners have been used as labor in public works. During the Depression, it is estimated that about a quarter of a million teens rode the rails. Estimates place the numbers of hoboes who were killed either by bulls or accidents between 6,500 and 8,500 a year. While not all railroad guards were brutal, they were known to shake down hoboes for money, maim, and even kill these itinerants.

I appreciate the insight I have been given into the restoration of vintage trailers by members of two groups, Midwest Glampers and the Sisters on the Fly. Also, Henry Wallace was very helpful about the 1937 Covered Wagon trailer.

Of course, I owe a great debt to input from my beta readers: Marcia, Ginge, brother Jim, son Pat and former classmate Lee. Thank you!

OTHER BOOKS BY THE AUTHOR

The award-winning Frannie Shoemaker Campground Mysteries:

Bats and Bones: (An IndieBRAG Medallion honoree) Frannie and Larry Shoemaker are retirees who enjoy weekend camping with their friends in state parks. They anticipate the usual hiking, campfires, good food, and interesting side trips among the bluffs of beautiful Bat Cave State Park until a dead body turns up. Confined in the campground and surrounded by strangers, Frannie is drawn into the investigation.

The Blue Coyote: (An IndieBRAG Medallion honoree and a 2013 Chanticleer CLUE finalist) Frannie and Larry Shoemaker love taking their grandchildren, Sabet and Joe, camping with them. But at Bluffs State Park, Frannie finds herself worrying more than usual about their safety, and when another young girl disappears from the campground in broad daylight, her fears increase. Accusations against Larry and her add to the cloud over their heads.

Peete and Repeat: (An IndieBRAG Medallion honoree, 2013 Chanticleer CLUE finalist, and 2014 Chanticleer Mystery and Mayhem finalist) A biking and camping trip to southeastern Minnesota turns into double trouble for Frannie Shoemaker and her friends as she deals with a canoeing mishap and a couple of bodies.

The Lady of the Lake: (An IndieBRAG Medallion honoree, 2014 Chanticleer CLUE finalist) A trip down memory lane is fine if you don't stumble on a body. Frannie Shoemaker and her friends camp at Old Dam Trail State Park near one of Donna Nowak's childhood homes and take in the county fair. But the present intrudes when a body surfaces. Donna becomes the focus of the investigation and Frannie wonders if the police shouldn't be looking closer at the victim's many enemies.

To Cache a Killer: Geocaching isn't supposed to be about finding dead bodies. But when retiree, Frannie Shoemaker go camping, standard definitions don't apply. A weekend in a beautiful state park in Iowa buzzes with fund-raising events, a search for Ninja turtles, a bevy of suspects, and lots of great food. But are the campers in the wrong place at the wrong time once too often?

A Campy Christmas: A Holiday novella. The Shoemakers and Ferraros plan to spend Christmas in Texas and then take a camping trip through the Southwest. But those plans are stopped cold when they hit a rogue ice storm in Missouri and they end up snowbound in a campground. And that's just the beginning. Includes recipes and winter camping tips.

The Space Invader: A cozy/thriller mystery! The starry skies over New Mexico, the "Land of Enchantment," may hold secrets of their own. The Shoemakers and the Ferraros, on an extended camping trip, find themselves picking up a souvenir they don't want and taking sidetrips they didn't plan on.

We are NOT Buying a Camper! A prequel to the Frannie Shoemaker Campground Mysteries. Frannie and Larry Shoemaker have busy jobs, two teenagers, and plenty of other demands on their time and sanity. Larry's sister and brother-in-law pester them to try camping for relaxation-- time to sit back, enjoy nature, and catch up on naps. After all, what could go wrong? Join Frannie as "RV there yet?" becomes "RV crazy?" and she learns that going back to nature doesn't necessarily mean a simpler life.

Happy Camper Tips and Recipes: All of the tips and recipes from the first four Frannie Shoemaker books in one convenient paperback or Kindle version that you can keep in your camping supplies!

About the Author

Karen Musser Nortman is the author of the Frannie Shoemaker Campground cozy mystery series, including the BRAGMedallion honoree, Bats and Bones. After previous incarnations as a secondary social studies teacher (22 years) and a test developer (18 years), she returned to her childhood dream of writing a novel.

Karen and her husband Butch originally tent camped when their children were young and switched to a travel trailer when sleeping on the ground lost its romantic adventure. They take frequent weekend jaunts with friends to parks in Iowa and surrounding states, plus occasional longer trips. Entertainment on these trips has ranged from geocaching and hiking/biking to barbecue contests, balloon fests, and buck skinners' rendezvous. Out of these trips came the Frannie Shoemaker Campground Mysteries and now *The Time Travel Trailer*.

More information is available on her website at www.karenmussernortman.com.